The Philosophical Detective's Last Case

Also by Bruce Hartman:

Perfectly Healthy Man Drops Dead

The Rules of Dreaming

The Muse of Violence

The Philosophical Detective

A Butterfly in Philadelphia

Big Data Is Watching You!
(also published as *I Am Not a Robot)*

Potlatch: A Comedy

The Devil's Chaplain

Parole

The Philosophical Detective Returns

The Philosophical Detective's Last Case

Bruce Hartman

Swallow Tail Press

The Philosophical Detective's Last Case

Published by Swallow Tail Press
Philadelphia, PA, USA
www.swallowtailpress.com

Cover illustration: Detail from "Newton" by William Blake

Also available in ebook format.

ISBN: 978-0-9997564-6-1

Author's Note

This is a work of fiction. Any resemblance to actual events or persons, living or dead, is entirely coincidental or used for fictional purposes only. I need hardly add that "Jorge Luis Borges" is a purely fictional product of my own imagination, not to be confused with the famous Argentine writer of the same name.

And I said, with rapture, Here is something I can study all my life, and never understand.

—Samuel Beckett, *Molloy*

Marriott Memory Care Center
Natick, Massachusetts

Here at the Marriott Memory Care Center, I don't have doctors or nurses. Like a run-down house that's been in the family too long, I have *caretakers*, puttering amateurs who busy themselves with maintenance and minor repairs, confident that the tenant will be moving out soon. They care for my memory as the gardener cares for the lawn, by saturating it with poisons and eradicating anything that sprouts up unexpectedly. Their mission is to make me remember what they think I ought to remember.

My secret revenge is to remember only the things *I* want to remember. Admittedly those memories are all from the distant past. What in my current life would any man in his right mind care to remember? The nauseating meals, the idiotic TV shows, the meaningless lists of words I'm required to recite to justify my caretakers' salaries? No, instead I spend my endless days and nights sifting through lost time for fragments of what has made my life worth living.

At the moment what I'm trying to recall is the last time I saw the great Argentinian poet and fabulist Jorge Luis Borges. When I first met him he was nearing seventy, world-renowned as the author of poems, essays, and the paradoxical prose pieces he called fictions. He was spending the 1967-68 academic year at Harvard; I was a 23-year-old graduate student at a nearby university who'd been dragooned into serving as his driver, guide and seeing-eye dog. Did I mention that he was blind? Yes, like Homer and Milton, he'd lost his sight and was forced to explore the mysteries of literature and philosophy within the labyrinth of his own mind. As it happened, he also had a lifelong interest in crime and detection. To the dismay of his academic hosts, he spent most of that year traipsing around New England solving a bizarre series of crimes. A few years later I helped him untangle his most celebrated case, the diabolical murders in the New York City morgue, and before we parted, not supposing that we would ever meet again, he anointed me as his narrator, his Watson as it were, the executor of his legacy as a detective. I'm determined to honor that designation by recording our last three adventures, the first of which is entitled, appropriately enough, "The Amnesia Ward." It's a tale of murder and deception which, for obvious reasons, is close to my heart. I'm anxious to write it down while I can still remember it.

I should mention that my family and my caretakers think my recollections of Borges are a fantasy. I have to admit that with my memories vanishing at an astonishing rate, the line between fact and fantasy has blurred, and so the stories I am about to relate may be false recollections or even fabrications. How do you really know whether what you remember is true? Borges taught me, or tried to teach me, that knowledge itself, especially the kind of knowledge we're most proud of, is a kind of fantasy. That was almost fifty years ago, but it's only since I've been locked up in the Memory Care Center that I've begun to understand what he meant.

For which I will be eternally grateful to my two loving daughters, who put me here.

The Amnesia Ward

These fragments I have shored against my ruins...
— T. Eliot, "The Waste Land."

One of Borges's most vexing cases centered on the conundrums of memory. Back in the 1970s they didn't have Memory Care Centers. What they did have, occupying the sixth floor of Saint Aloysius University Medical Center in Boston, was a separate, all-but-forgotten unit of the Department of Neurology devoted to memory loss and related conditions, popularly known as the Amnesia Ward. That was where, one balmy April afternoon—after an urgent call from the attending physician—I found the man I knew as Jorge Luis Borges. It was three years since we'd parted in New York.

He had been attending a literary conference at Boston University, which he must have found boring. During a break he decided to step outside for a breath of fresh air, guided only by the red-tipped cane he called his walking stick. Stumbling off the curb into Commonwealth Avenue, he triggered a major traffic pile-up that resulted in a squad of ambulances rushing him and a dozen others to the emergency room at St. Aloysius. In the confusion no one seemed to notice that he was blind, a foreigner, and seventy-four years old. When an intern, checking for head injury, asked him who the President was, he replied, "The man whose name I will not utter." (He meant Perón, not Nixon.) When the doctor asked if he could remember his mother's maiden name, he brandished his walking stick and challenged him to "settle this outside."

"And what is your occupation, sir?"

"Late Director of the National Library of Argentina."

That clinched it. Without delay he was wheeled up to the Amnesia Ward, just in time for his afternoon nap. He carried no identification, but in his pocket they found a note from me, which included my telephone number, suggesting that we meet for lunch while he was in Boston. The attending physician, Dr. Leona Marlow, called me at once.

By the time I arrived Borges was having a grand time chatting with one of the nurses, Sister Joseph. As soon as she left the room, he admonished me to keep quiet about who he was and whether he had anything wrong with him. He intended to stay in the hospital for a bit of rest until they forced him to leave.

"Do they know who you are?" I asked him.

He shook his head. "They think I'm Borges."

"Well, you are Borges, aren't you?"

"Only as an impostor. The real Borges is a figment of my imagination."

If I hadn't known him, I might have thought he was crazy. But for Borges this was business as usual, with a twist even Chuang Tzu's butterfly hadn't dreamed of: he was an impostor pretending not to be who he pretended to be.

The Amnesia Ward was like an alternative universe where the usual rules of time and space did not apply. Dozens of patients roamed the halls, most of them tormented souls of the man-who-mistook-his-wife-for-a-hat variety, who knew something was wrong but were powerless to overcome it. For others—accident survivors, stroke victims, sufferers of degenerative disease—there was no past, or no future, or in some cases, I suppose, no present. I never thought amnesia had undone so many. What had any of them done to deserve such afflictions? I was still young, not yet midway down the path of life, and this glimpse into a hellish future (for that's what it seemed) upset me. On that path I'd known my share of near misses, narrow escapes, and hard knocks, stretches of time when I couldn't distinguish between memory and imagination, or when my sense of self had slipped away. In my present state—recently married, expecting a child, struggling with my first real job—there was serious work to be done, in place of the dreamlike musing I'd indulged in for so long. The aging poet, deliberately or not, had lured me to that refuge of unimaginable beings. Would he be able to guide me through it and back into the ordinary world?

It was an old red-brick hospital built in the 1920s. The rooms in the Amnesia Ward clustered around a large open lobby with the nurses' station in the middle, comfortable chairs in alcoves along the walls, and a common room with a TV and tables for playing cards or checkers. The patients were encouraged to walk around and interact with each other, so that they could be observed in the activities of everyday life. When I stepped off the elevator, I saw a man in the throes of what appeared to be an epileptic seizure. He writhed on the floor biting the carpet and nobody paid him the least bit of attention.

"Aren't you going to help this man?" I called to one of the nurses.

"Oh, don't mind Alonso," she said. "He faked a heart attack this morning."

Borges shared the room with three other patients—introduced as Ivan, Walter, and Patrick—each of whom suffered from his own unique memory disturbance. The four men, fully dressed, lounged in a row on padded recliners which converted into beds, separated by small tables holding lamps and trays for medications. The department, I later learned, followed a new therapeutic model similar to group therapy (after all, this was the 1970s). The patients were encouraged to talk openly about their condition with each other as well as with the doctors and staff, who interacted with each of them in front of all the others. There were no secrets on the Amnesia Ward.

Along the wall opposite the recliners stood a row of chairs for visitors. There was a calendar on the wall and a big clock with a sweeping second hand. I pulled one of the chairs over to sit beside Borges, who looked his usual dapper self in a dark suit and tie. Before I sat down he introduced me to the other three patients. Ivan was short and dark, exuding an aura of despondency, his deep-set eyes animated but strangely vacant. In Central Europe after the war, I later learned, he had been a memory artist, that is, a professional mnemonist who performed feats of memory for paying audiences in music halls and traveling circuses. He could memorize telephone books, city directories, train schedules, anything they put in front of him. Now he spoke in meaningless strings of words and his memory appeared to be as empty as the expressionless eyes he focused on the wall clock's relentless second hand.

Then there was Walter, a retired actuary who'd worked forty years at the John Hancock life insurance company. With beetling eyebrows, translucent gray eyes, and black-framed glasses sliding down his nose, he certainly looked the part. "When I went to business school," he told me, "I planned to be an accountant, but my advisor said I didn't have the personality for it. So I became an actuary. Never regretted it once in the forty years, three months and twenty-two days I worked at John Hancock."

Walter suffered from a rare neurological disorder. A blow to the occipital region had turned him into a kind of idiot savant. He couldn't remember his address, his date of birth, or his shoe size, but he had a vast library of actuarial tables at his command. In a heartbeat he could calculate the life expectancy of every man, woman and child on the planet, at any point in their lives, within a two-day margin of error. Oddly enough, this uncanny talent had led him to a discovery which, if widely accepted, would have meant the end of the life insurance industry. We would learn about that later.

Naturally Borges was delighted to have such an eccentric pair of roommates as Ivan and Walter. But the most remarkable patient in the group was a florid, jovial man of about fifty-five whose name tag identified him as Patrick McColgan. Patrick had a slightly lopsided face and a fresh scar on the top of his balding head; he had been transferred from the post-surgical unit just the day before. He talked and joked incessantly, filling the room with laughter which in any place other than a hospital might have been called infectious. His uninhibited happiness had made him a big hit with Borges and the other patients, and he was eager to talk about how he'd achieved it. "I can't remember anything," he chuckled, "but they say I tried to blow my brains out with a .22 caliber pistol. Apparently I'm sitting at my desk and I stick the muzzle in my mouth and pull the trigger, but I don't aim it right. You're supposed to aim toward the back and instead, klutz that I am, I aim it upward. Can you believe that?" He let out a peal of laughter that brought sympathetic guffaws from around the room. "So the bullet goes straight up through my head and comes out here"—he pointed to the scar on his head—"and lodges in the wainscoting behind my desk. And on the way up it sort of cuts my brain in half, so that—wait'll you hear this!—I can't remember why I wanted to kill myself in the first place! Dr. Marlow wouldn't like to hear me say this, but I'm as happy as a Gloucester clam!"

"You're right about that," chimed an authoritative female voice. We all turned to find a tall, square-shouldered woman of about forty-five beaming at us from the other end of the room, where she had apparently been standing all along. She wore a white lab coat, open in the front, over a gray dress that matched her imperious eyes. This, I learned, was Dr. Leona Marlow, the attending physician.

"We don't want to hear how happy you are from losing your memory, Patrick," she said. "Our mission here is to help you recover it. *That's* what will make you happy."

Patrick replied with a twinkle in his eyes: "How would that make me happy?"

Good question, I thought. Why would the world's happiest man want to know why he tried to blow his brains out?

"As we discussed yesterday in our therapy session," Dr. Marlow smiled, "how can you know who you are—how can you even *be* who you are?—if you don't have your memories?"

"I'm sure I'm better off without them," Patrick laughed. "I'm about as happy as a man can be."

There's a killjoy in every crowd. In this case it was the hospital chaplain, Father Geraghty, who had glided in behind Dr. Marlow. He was a wiry, bright-eyed little man resembling a leprechaun, with a broad forehead, a tea-spout nose, and a razor-sharp voice honed by decades of disputation. "Happiness is highly overrated," he said, wagging his forefinger at Patrick. "It may ease your time in this world, but it won't absolve you from mortal sin. I refer to the sin of suicide—which is the worst sin of all."

"I understand that, Father," Patrick said, stifling his mirth. "But as you can see, I didn't succeed in killing myself. Don't I get some credit for that?"

"Poor marksmanship is not a defense. You committed the sin when you decided to shoot yourself, and again when you pulled the trigger. Your only hope of salvation is to repent."

"All right." Patrick put on a sober face and crossed himself. "Forgive me, Father, for I have sinned. I repent. I sincerely repent."

"Very well, my son," the priest said. His eyes gleamed with cunning. "What specific act do you repent of?"

"Well, shooting myself."

"Do you remember doing it?"

"Absolutely not."

"Do you remember deciding to do it?"

He shook his head and chuckled nervously. "No."

"Do you remember the reasons that led you to do it?"

"No, not at all."

There was a long, awkward silence. Beads of sweat trickled down Patrick's forehead and moistened his cheeks. His hand trembled as he wiped them off with his sleeve.

Father Geraghty smirked as he watched Patrick twist in the trap he'd set for him. "If you don't remember anything about it, how can you repent?"

All the happiness had drained from Patrick's face.

"I'm afraid a repentance under such circumstances would be false and ineffective," the priest said with an air of regret.

"Then I'm going to Hell?"

"Without a doubt. Unless you can recover the memory of what you did and why you did it."

Dr. Marlow edged forward and squeezed the patient's hand. "That's what the medical team is here for, Patrick," she said. "We'll use every resource at our disposal to restore your memories. No effort will be spared."

Patrick was no longer the happiest man in world. Not even the first or second runner up. His chances of reclaiming that title were on a par with the Red Sox winning the World Series.

"So there's hope?" he mumbled.

Father Geraghty nodded dubiously. "A murder has been committed," he said. "The murder of your immortal soul."

"And I did it."

"Unfortunately, yes."

While this inquisition proceeded, the room had filled with visitors. They were all there to see Patrick: his wife Lorraine, his daughter Daphne, his son Andrew, and his business partner, Brian Daley. Lorraine—Patrick's second wife and not the mother of his children—wore pink lipstick and an icy smile. Her lips were thin, her chin taut, her cheeks stretched tight as a drum—in the war against time she was fighting for every inch of disputed territory. The way she and Brian Daley avoided looking at each other, it was obvious that they were sleeping together.

Brian didn't strike me as the sort of man I'd want to trust with my business or my wife. He wore a dress shirt open at the neck, rhinestone-studded cufflinks, and three heavy class rings, probably from schools he'd been expelled from. His long hair and sideburns (the fashion in those days) gave him the appearance of a disgraced Civil War general.

Patrick later told us what little he could remember about his daughter. Daphne was in her late twenties, an unemployed art-school graduate whose tastes ran to expensive clothes, vintage wines, and exotic destinations. Physically stunning, she'd attracted a succession of starving artists, avant-garde ne'er-do-wells, and minimalist no-accounts. She and her parents had finally become estranged over her relationship with an older, twice-divorced abstract expressionist named Frank Serafini, whom Patrick and Lorraine had refused to meet. In a bitter moment (which he regretted and planned to rectify) Patrick had told her that if she married Frank Serafini she would be disinherited. The estrangement continued even during the hospital visit. Daphne seemed disappointed not to find her father drawing his last breath.

Finally there was Andrew, the twenty-year-old junior at Boston College. He spent most of the visit bobbing his head to music only he could hear. I think he might have smoked too much dope while he was supposed to be playing lacrosse.

For all of us, I think, the arrival of Patrick's family came as a revelation that put his case in a whole new light. When you met the people he was closest to, you began to understand why the world's happiest man had tried to kill himself. I felt like an unwelcome guest, though of course I was there to see Borges. The old fantasist had been uncharacteristically quiet since I arrived. I was about to suggest that we go for a stroll around the Amnesia Ward when Patrick grabbed his wife's hand and pulled her toward him. "I'm going to Hell," he blurted, "unless I can remember why I tried to kill myself."

"That's probably where you belong, dear," Lorraine reassured him with a tight smile, untangling herself from his grip. Daphne nodded vehemently and cursed him under her breath.

Patrick seemed on the verge of tears.

It was Walter, the actuary, who came to the rescue. "Don't worry, Patrick," he said. "I know why you did it."

"You do?"

"Money problems," Walter said. "Nine out of ten times—89.7% of the time, to be precise—when a man your age kills himself, it's over money."

Patrick appealed to his wife. "Was I having money problems?"

"No, dear. The business had its best year ever. Isn't that right, Brian?"

Brian grunted assent without letting his eyes meet Lorraine's.

Walter held his ground. "Then it must have been covered by the other 10.3 percent."

"And what is that?" Patrick asked. Sweat streamed off his forehead like the sand in an hourglass trickling out the last minutes of his life.

"What do *you* think?"

Patrick glanced once more at his wife, then at his daughter, but neither offered to help. "You've got me."

"Women," Walter said. "The other ten percent is women."

Something told me it was time to get Borges out of that room. I helped him sit up and hoisted him to a standing position as he paid his compliments to Patrick's family with his usual punctilio. Gripping his walking stick in one hand and my elbow in the other, he let me guide him into the hall at the pace of a snail racing a tortoise. I felt as if I'd stumbled into a paradox about the impossibility of motion.

Our glacial progress toward the lobby gave Borges a chance to collect his thoughts about the scene we'd just witnessed. "If you read Dante's *Inferno*," he said, "you'll find that the lost souls Dante consigned to Hell had one thing in common: they could all remember what they did to get there. Otherwise how could they have told him their stories? And how could they suffer throughout all eternity for their sins if they couldn't remember them?"

"I've often wondered about that," I lied.

"Meanwhile, the blissful souls in Paradise have no memories at all. But now the wily priest, Father Geraghty, has stood Dante's logic on its head. According to him, Patrick is damned for his sins precisely *because* he can't remember them."

"Maybe somebody ought to notify the Spanish Inquisition."

"It will surely be one of the most unusual investigations in the annals of crime."

I was surprised by his reference to crime. Yes, suicide is a crime, but it's a victimless crime, isn't it? For a believer like

Patrick, eternal damnation should be punishment enough until they think of something worse.

"You don't believe in Hell, do you?" I asked Borges.

"Only Hell on earth," he said, "which seems to be everywhere. But as a detective I must put my personal beliefs aside in order to concentrate on the case."

"What case?"

"The murder case, of course."

"But there hasn't been a murder," I objected.

"There will be. I have no doubt about that."

Murder? As a self-styled detective, Borges saw murders lurking around every corner, apparently even before they had been committed. And I had to admit that the crowd in that room—Patrick's family, his eccentric fellow patients, the wily priest, even Dr. Marlow and Sister Joseph, could have stocked an Agatha Christie novel with enough suspects to baffle Hercule Poirot. Borges refused to identify the victim; his logic he explained only later.

I could only hope that fate would spare Patrick, who had enough to worry about without being murdered. The precariousness of his position—would he leave the hospital as the world's happiest man or a lost soul in Hell?—came into stark relief when Dr. Marlow, Father Geraghty, and Sister Joseph emerged into the hall, heads bowed together in earnest consultation. Against the combined forces of modern science and medieval superstition, the man didn't have a fighting chance. "Patrick's memory should be coming back in a couple of days," Dr. Marlow was saying. "We need him to remember exactly what drove him to suicide."

"It was the family, obviously," Father Geraghty said. "Did you see how the daughter looked at him?"

"The question is, why did his life become unbearable? Was it the torment of living with that family? Or some kind of existential despair? We need to get him to remember all that or we won't be able to help him."

"The devil's in the details," the priest agreed.

The doctor signaled the nurse to make a notation in the patient's chart. "Painful as they may be, we need to bring back as many of those memories as we possibly can."

"When he remembers everything, he'll be able to repent."

"And we can notch one more cure for the team."

"And then what?" Sister Joseph asked naively.

"Then we'll have to put him on suicide watch."

After what seemed like hours Borges and I reached the large open lobby in front of the nurses' station, where we found ourselves in the midst of a medical emergency. The patient who'd been gnawing the carpet when I arrived had fallen into a coma. He was a tall, powerfully-built man with a manicured appearance, and now he lay motionless on the floor, his tongue lolling, his eyes fixed blankly on the ceiling. In that position, possibly because of his pointed black mustache, he reminded me of Salvador Dalí. A young intern—his name tag identified him as Dr. Ginzburg—knelt beside him, holding his wrist slightly elevated as he took his pulse. Sister Joseph stood nearby with his chart.

"Who is this patient?" Dr. Ginzburg asked Sister Joseph.

"Alonso Quijano," she said, reading from the chart. "Admitted last night with a bump on his head. Couldn't remember how it happened. The night staff observed episodes of paranoia, hallucination, and delusion. So far today he's exhibited symptoms of heart attack and epileptic seizure. And now a diabetic coma."

The intern released Mr. Quijano's hand and it remained hanging in the air. "What's the diagnosis?"

"He's a Munchausen."

Dr. Ginzburg laughed out loud. "OK, get him back to bed. We'll hold him a couple more days for observation. Who knows what else he'll come up with?"

"A Munchausen?" Borges muttered in astonishment.

Sister Joseph leaned closer and lowered her voice. "It's what they call a person who fakes a serious illness to get into the hospital."

"The man must be mad."

She allowed herself a wry smile. "Or pretending to be."

"They amount to the same thing," Borges nodded. "Who but a madman would pretend to be mad?"

2.

By this time it was late afternoon and I was starting to worry about Borges. When he traveled he always had people looking after him, often an assistant provided by the university he was visiting. After he disappeared from the conference that morning there must have been a dozen people searching for him, who by now would be in a panic. Evidently no one had connected him with the accident or the ambulance that whisked him away.

"We need to get in touch with the university," I told him as we sat down in the lobby. "Who's your contact person there?"

"I don't approve of that usage of 'contact,'" he said. "'Contact person' even less."

"All right. Who's taking care of you?"

"You are."

"I mean who was taking care of you before the accident?"

He replied with a mischievous smile. "Has there been an accident?"

Oh, I almost forgot. This was the Amnesia Ward, where everyone was entitled to his own oblivion. In that surreal atmosphere, I was starting to feel anxious and confused. I had a pregnant wife, the faithful Katie, who'd be waiting for me at home. I'd just started a new job, from which I couldn't afford to be absent another day. Not long before, thanks to a lovely librarian I met in New York, I'd overcome my lifelong sense of not knowing who I was—an achievement imperiled by renewed association with Borges, who believed, or pretended to believe, that everyone is an impostor. He'd told me more than once that personal identity is rooted in the continuity of memory, which is an illusion. What did that say about Ivan, Walter and Patrick, who'd lost large chunks of their memories? How could we know who any of them really were? Was Patrick the world's happiest man or the most miserable? Was Ivan a melancholy genius or a mindless shell?

Was Walter an idiot savant or just a plain idiot? Who among them (if Borges's prediction was correct) would turn out to be a murderer, and who a victim? Borges himself was a kind of Munchausen, faking amnesia to stay in the hospital. Or was that just his way of concealing a real impairment? I decided to call the Police Department to see if he had been reported missing.

"Are you okay sitting here while I make a couple of phone calls?" I asked him.

"Of course. And while you're at it, why don't you pick up a bottle of whisky?"

"Whisky? Are you serious?" By whisky, Borges meant scotch.

"It's almost cocktail hour."

Sister Joseph happened to walk by as he said that. "I'll see if the other gentlemen would like to join you," she said, as if cocktail hour was a normal part of hospital routine.

"Is there a telephone I can use?" I asked her.

"There's a pay phone down in the main lobby."

Incredible as it may seem, in those days you didn't carry a telephone around in your pocket. You had to find a pay phone, squeeze yourself into a glass booth that only Superman could turn around in, and feed nickels, dimes and quarters into an apparatus that was usually out of order. If you didn't know the number you had to ask an operator for assistance, an interaction that typically led to a dial tone or a busy signal. I found a general number for the university and left a message that Borges was safe in St. Aloysius and I would call back in the morning. Then I called Katie and tried to explain what I was doing, which didn't elicit a sympathetic response (she had always considered Borges a charlatan). Then I called the missing persons bureau at the Police Department, where the receptionist, a friendly lady with an Irish brogue, put me on hold until my coins ran out. I gave up and went looking for a bottle of scotch.

Returning to the hospital thirty minutes later, a fifth of Dewar's concealed under my jacket, I waited for the elevator and came face to face with Patrick's family as the door opened in front of me. It was like a glimpse into one of the back alleys of Hell. The wife and daughter faced ahead with tight-clenched, flushed faces, as if they'd just tried to tear each other's eyes out. The son, Andrew, stared at me like a brain-starved zombie. The business partner, Brian Daley, stood behind them, his lips curled in a derisive smirk. For me it was one of those disorienting moments when you encounter someone you've met in a different setting. I smiled and stepped aside to let them pass. They didn't smile back.

Upstairs in the Amnesia Ward I found Borges holding court at a card table in the common room. Patrick and Walter sat on either side of him; directly opposite sat Ivan, along with Dr. Marlow, who had pulled up a chair beside Ivan. They were all waiting for me to arrive with the whisky. Sister Joseph had set the table with cocktail glasses, a bottle of club soda, and a bucket of ice. Borges played the host, urging drinks on the others, though he himself drank hardly at all. Patrick was as jolly as ever, Walter guarded and calculating,

Ivan his usual furtive, silent self, staring at the clock on the wall. Dr. Marlow was talking to Borges, apparently in the middle of explaining Ivan's condition.

"Ivan has a rare memory disorder," she said. "Any attempt to exercise his once-prodigious memory triggers off a stream of free association that pushes him farther and farther away from reality." She turned to Ivan and studied his dark, hollow eyes. "Ivan"—she pointed at me—"do you remember Nick Martin coming to your room this afternoon?"

Ivan cleared his throat. "1:45 and 13 seconds."

"That is about when I got there," I confirmed.

"He never takes his eyes off the clock," the doctor said.

He tore his eyes off the clock and peered at me. "Sunlight, shirt, window, red, yellow, green, stripe, plaid, eyes, eyelid, blinking, glancing, face, breeze, dust, dragon, fire, tail, Dr. Borges, Michigan, Patrick, Walter, male, age, 10.8%, wolverines, Great Lakes, cars, trucks—"

"That's enough, Ivan," Dr. Marlow broke in gently, touching his hand. She turned to Borges: "This is the way it goes. If you were to ask him what happened at 1:46, he would launch into another free association that would take him equally far into the weeds. It's just gibberish."

"I doubt that very much," Borges said. "The first string of words was probably about Nick's clothing, which of course I can't see. Nick, are you wearing a red, yellow and green plaid or striped necktie?"

I didn't need to check my tie since I only had one. "I sure am," I answered.

"And when you walked past the window, was there a breeze or a gust of wind that might have blown the dust in a pattern resembling a dragon?"

"If there was, I don't remember it. I probably didn't even notice it."

"As to the rest," Borges said, "I can tell you where that came from. I had described a recent trip to Michigan, and Patrick was trying to remember if he'd ever been to Michigan, and Walter pointed out that there was only a 10.8% chance that a male resident of Boston of Patrick's age had ever visited the Wolverine State. The discussion reminded him of the Great Lakes and the automobile industry and its cars, trucks, etc. So you see, it's not fair to say that his memory is impaired. With equal justice you might say it has been enhanced. He remembers everything in such exhaustive detail that we can't even recognize them as memories."

The doctor shook her head and smiled. "If that's true," she said, "you've discovered a memory disorder that's unknown to medical science."

Borges beamed with apparent pride, as if he'd missed her irony. "You mentioned that Ivan was once a professional mnemonist. What have you been able to learn about that?"

"He studied a mnemonic technique that is well known in Europe. It involves associating what you want to remember with a set of vivid, unforgettable images that you've already embedded in your mind in a certain order."

"Ah! The *ars memorativa* invented by the ancient Greek poet Simonides."

"You're familiar with the technique?"

"Cicero describes a famous case where Simonides used it to perform some of the earliest recorded detective work. He'd been hired to recite his poetry at a banquet, and when the host balked at paying him, he stepped outside; a few minutes later the roof collapsed on the banquet hall, crushing and mutilating the host and all his guests beyond recognition. By using his novel memory technique at the behest of the victims' relatives, Simonides was able to collect more than his stipulated fee by identifying the corpses based on where they had been sitting."

"A dubious accomplishment," I observed, "since there was no way of knowing which corpse was which, other than through Simonides's identification. So although he was undoubtedly an accomplished poet, as a detective he might have been a complete charlatan."

"Or something worse," Borges smiled. "There's evidence in Cicero's account that Simonides might have been complicit in the building's collapse. Of course"—he waved his hand like a magician pulling a pigeon from the air—"there's always been a suspicion that the detective causes the crime."

A low growl quavered over the table as Ivan clenched his fists with his eyes cast down. He muttered a random series of words in a halting Central European accent that was the perfect complement to his furtive, hollow eyes.

Dr. Marlow shook her head. "You get the sense that he's struggling to remember something from his distant past, possibly something that happened in his childhood or during the war."

"Or maybe he's just trying to put into words something he experienced ten seconds ago," Borges said. "For a man without a memory, there wouldn't be any difference."

The doctor stood up and excused herself. "I have some paperwork to do," she said. "Ivan, you stay here and enjoy the cocktail party. Maybe these gentlemen can help put you back in touch with your memories."

"Or help you drown them," Patrick laughed, topping Ivan's glass with scotch. "If you've got any left. I sure as hell don't!"

After the doctor left there was a long, troubled silence, as each of us tried to imagine how we could lighten Ivan's burden. Each of us, I should say, except Patrick, who along with his memory must have lost his empathy for others. He cracked jokes and smiled his happy smile, as if Ivan's predicament meant nothing to him; and for a moment, I'm ashamed to admit, I found myself siding with the diabolical priest in consigning him to perpetual torment. But no, I told myself, poor Patrick's only sin was the sin of happiness; he meant no harm, probably wasn't even aware of what he was doing. How could I blame the world's happiest man for missing the parts of his brain that make other men miserable?

I should probably exclude Walter as well from those sympathizing with Ivan's plight. I'd watched him out of the corner of my eye as his black-framed eyeglasses slid down his nose at regular intervals, reaching a point just above the nostrils every fifteen seconds, whereupon he would push them back up to the bridge and the cycle would begin again. Keeping those glasses up was a Sisyphean task which I suspect he was fated to repeat for as long as he lived. After a life in the insurance industry, he was as inured to suffering and misfortune as a dealer in Las Vegas. Whatever happened was a predictable stopping point on the ever-revolving wheel of fortune.

"There's a kind of amnesia that is the loss not of memory but of forgetting," Borges said. "Do we have our memories, or do they have us? If they could forget us, maybe we could forget them."

Ivan cleared his throat and lowered his eyes.

"In medieval times," Borges went on, "Simonides's technique was extolled by St. Thomas Aquinas and other churchmen. They used it to memorize scripture, to rehearse their interminable sermons, to recall the glories of the Earthly Paradise before Adam's fall. But it also had its dark side. To such men Dante's *Inferno*—with its horrific imagery of sinners and eternal punishments—was an elaborate mnemonic device. They called it Remembering Hell."

3.

"We all have our private Hells," Borges said, "to remember or forget." He took a sip of whisky and aimed his sightless gaze at Patrick. "For example: Patrick, tell us again about the day you shot yourself."

"I don't remember anything about it," Patrick said cheerfully.

"Then tell us what you told me before. You remember that, don't you?"

He shook his head, apparently forgetting that Borges was blind.

"One of my oddities," Borges said, "and it developed after I lost my sight, is that I can remember any literary creation, any ordered form of words, with verbatim accuracy. So in that sense I can do your remembering for you. Earlier this afternoon, you gave us an account of your suicide attempt. Do you remember that?"

"No, I can't say that I do."

"All right, then. I'll tell you what you said in your exact words." Borges took a moment to collect his thoughts. "You said"—and the words sounded ludicrous coming out of Borges's mouth—"'I'm sitting at my desk and I stick the muzzle in my mouth and pull the trigger, but I don't aim it right. You're supposed to aim toward the back and instead, klutz that I am, I aim it upward. Can you believe that? So the bullet goes straight up through my head and comes out here and lodges in the wainscoting behind my desk. And on the way up—'"

He cut himself off and asked Patrick, "Do you remember saying that?"

Patrick shook his head. "Nope."

"Can anyone tell me what's wrong with this picture?"

We all stared at Borges in a paralyzed silence. No one ventured a guess.

"All right, I'll tell you," he said. "Everyone knows that if you want to shoot yourself you must aim toward the back of your mouth. Instead the bullet was fired upward and exited through the top of Patrick's head *and lodged in the wainscoting behind his desk.* Not in the ceiling, but in the wainscoting, which is to say in the wall. For the bullet to lodge in the wall he couldn't have been sitting upright in his desk chair. He must have been lying back with his face up when the gun was fired. Obviously that was because someone stuck a gun in his mouth and pushed him backwards in the chair before pulling the trigger."

Another long silence as we all struggled to make sense of what Borges had said. Somewhere a clock was ticking.

"Then... what you're saying," Patrick stammered, with the faintest glimmer of hope in his eyes, "is that I didn't shoot myself?"

"That's right," Borges said. "Somebody else shot you. Somebody who wanted to kill you."

"But who would have done that?"

Walter pushed his glasses to the top of his nose and waited for them to begin their descent. "Probably someone you know," he said, fixing Patrick in his actuarial gaze. Behind his translucent eyes you could almost see the adding-machine gears turning, powered by his monomania for statistical prognostication. "Most murderers know their victims. In fact, 54.3% of them are members of the victim's family."

"The wife?" Patrick gulped nervously.

"34.7% of the time."

"A son? A daughter?"

"We don't break it down that way when we're writing a policy. Every unhappy family is unhappy in its own way."

"A wife's lover?"

With that question, Patrick's fate was sealed. It was as if he'd let it slip that he was a sky-diver or a three-pack-a-day smoker. Walter peered back at him with a tiny, triumphant smile. "Does your wife have a lover?"

"Just speaking hypothetically."

"Because if she does"—the actuary set his glass down hard, signaling that his judgment was final—"you're uninsurable." He pushed his eyeglasses up and turned away. "I'm sorry, Patrick."

We all knew what that meant. In Walter's world, "uninsurable" meant Rejected. Hopeless. Doomed.

"Now what?" Patrick sputtered.

"The second attempt usually comes within a week. 68.5% of the time, to be exact."

"In this case we should expect it sooner than that," Borges said. "It'll come before you recover your memories and are able to identify the would-be killer. Dr. Marlow says that should happen within a couple of days."

Now I understood how Borges knew there would be a murder. The victim would be Patrick, the killer whoever flubbed the first attempt—and it would happen soon.

The world's happiest man had been having a bad day. First being assured that he was going to Hell, and now, it seemed, actually being there. Someone close to him had tried to blow his brains out and would return to finish the job within a couple of days. He must have felt that he was already in the company of the damned. And the rest of us couldn't offer him any comfort. Sad-eyed Ivan, tottering on the abyss every time he tried to tap his memory. Walter the actuary, half mad if not 99.5% there, doomed to push his glasses up his nose until the end of time (which, as he was about to demonstrate, would never come). And myself, who should have abandoned all hope when I entered the Amnesia Ward, instead of letting Borges guide me through that labyrinth of lost souls.

To make matters worse, at this moment the diabolical chaplain, Father Geraghty, burst onto the scene, pushing Alonso Quijano, the muscular Munchausen (whom we'd last seen sprawled on the floor in a diabetic coma), into the lobby in a wheelchair. "So he can join the fun," the priest explained, adding with a wink that Alonso's current diagnosis, myasthenia gravis, would probably preclude him from doing so.

"And what, may I ask, is myasthenia gravis?" Borges asked.

"It's a chronic neuromuscular disease characterized by extreme muscle weakness," replied Sister Joseph, who'd sidled in behind Father Geraghty. Alonso confirmed the diagnosis by attempting to raise his lolling head. He peered back at Borges behind drooping eyelids as the rest of his face sagged.

"There's good news and bad news," Patrick told the priest. "I didn't shoot myself. Somebody—probably a close friend or family member—attempted to murder me. That's the good news. The bad news is they'll probably try again before I get my memory back, which will be within a couple of days."

Father Geraghty greeted the news with a thin smile. "In this sinful world we take our comforts where we find them."

"At least I won't be going to Hell."

"Perhaps not."

"But I didn't try to kill myself!"

The priest reminded me of the clerk at the Department of Motor Vehicles when I tried to explain why my registration fee should be waived after my car was totaled. "Eternal damnation isn't so easily overturned," he said, avoiding Patrick's eyes. "There are processes and procedures that must be followed, an interest in finality—"

"But I can't be sent to Hell for something I didn't do!"

Father Geraghty's eyes blazed like the bonfire of the vanities. "At the very least you have committed the sin of presumption," he declared. "The sin of presuming to know God's will before He has exercised it. A very grave sin indeed—a mortal sin—and not easily forgiven, since the expectation of forgiveness is part of the sin."

Surely this was a madhouse, I thought, and I was witnessing a debate between two lunatics. What could a sane person do in such circumstances? I glanced at Borges (admittedly a poor choice), hoping for guidance. He gazed blindly ahead with a Buddha-like serenity, lost in his own thoughts. Was there no one who could stop this madness?

Fortunately a third lunatic waited his turn to speak. "Don't listen to him, Patrick!" Walter shouted, springing to his feet. "There's no such thing as Hell!"

"Of course there is," the priest smirked. "Hell is other people."

"There can't be a Hell," Walter insisted, "because death is an illusion." He aimed his fierce glare at Father Geraghty. "Foisted on us by your boss, the Great Illusionist!"

"You're insane," the priest scoffed, though he sounded unconvinced. After all, wasn't his particular form of magic based on turning death into an illusion?

"I can prove it mathematically," Walter declared.

He loosened his cuffs and raised his arms to prove that he had nothing up his sleeves. Then, reaching in a pocket, he pulled out a green eye-shade, which he slipped over his beetling brow, an actuarial wizard preparing to conjure eternal life.

He called for a volunteer and foolishly I raised my hand.

"Stand up, please," he told me. "What's your name?"

"Dominick Martin."

Pulling out a pen and a pocket notebook, he scrutinized me from head to toe as if evaluating me for a life insurance policy. "White male," he muttered. "Non-smoker, I assume. How old are you?"

"I'll be thirty next month."

He jotted a note. "All right. Your life expectancy right now is 51 years, 3 months and 5 days."

I did some quick mental math. "Then I'll live until I'm 81?"

"In all likelihood. But as you get older, your life expectancy increases, as measured at the time of calculation. So in forty years, when you're 70, your life expectancy will be 18 years, 6 months and 14 days."

"That gets me to 88. I've gained 7 years!"

"Correct. Now let's say you ask me again when you're 87. Your life expectancy then will be 5 years, 8 months and 29 days."

"I'm up to 92."

"Exactly. And at 91, your life expectancy will be 4 years, 2 months, and 20 days. That puts you a little over 95."

He ventured a sly smile and pushed his glasses up his nose. "And there's no reason to stop there. Your life expectancy will always be a little higher than whatever age you actually are. If that wasn't true"—he glanced at Borges as if to make sure he was still alive—"you'd already be dead."

I sensed some flaw in his logic, but who would quibble with eternal life? "Does this mean I'll live forever?"

Walter nodded sagely. His glasses slid down and he pushed them back up, a process which, he evidently believed, would go on for all eternity. "We all will," he said. "The interval gets shorter and shorter with each calculation. Eventually it gets down to minutes, seconds, infinitesimal fractions of a second—but it never gets to zero. Death is an illusion."

Death an illusion! That would have been electrifying news under any circumstances. Coming from Walter it was all the more astonishing. After mankind's relentless, millennia-long quest for immortality, encompassing the Egyptian mummies, the Christian mysteries, the Philosopher's Stone (to cite just a few examples), after eons of effort by priests, theologians, philosophers, mystics, shamans, and sorcerers to conquer death or explain it away, who would have thought that the secret of eternal life would be revealed by an insurance actuary in a green eye-shade? For a heartbeat or two, everyone in that room—myself, Borges, Ivan, Patrick, Father Geraghty, Sister Joseph, even Alonso Quijano, who struggled to keep his drooping eyelids open—must have been tempted by Walter's specious logic. This was immortality he was talking about, not some footnote in the book of the cosmos, not some trivial paradox that could be skimmed over and forgotten—this was the Big If, the ultimate question of life and death, and like countless others before us, we were reluctant to close our eyes to the slightest glimmer of hope. Of course our rational minds told us that eternal life could not be achieved through tricky math developed by the insurance industry. And yet, and yet...

Did I say everyone in that room must have been tempted by Walter's vision? I should have excluded Borges, who had heard it all before. "Twenty-five centuries ago," he said, "Zeno of Elea showed that if Achilles and a tortoise were paired in a race, and the tortoise given a head start, Achilles would never catch up to the tortoise. Thus he proved that change is impossible, to which you have added the welcome corollary that death is an illusion. We all must be greatly relieved."

"I have no fear of death," Walter said.

"I do," Patrick said. "But what kind of life can I have when I can't remember anything?"

"Memory, too, is an illusion," Borges reassured him. "I once (or was it twice?) refuted the existence of time, based on the metaphysical idealism of Bishop Berkeley and the skepticism of David Hume. Berkeley said the physical world exists only in a perceiving mind. Hume went further and denied the existence of a 'self' underlying the mind's perceptions. Neither philosopher questioned the existence of time as a continuous background of existence. Yet by what right, I have asked, do we insist on continuous time? Ancient texts teach us that yesterday's man died in the man of today, and today's man dies in the man of tomorrow. The man of the present moment is the only one who has even a fleeting existence. To insist on time existing outside the present moment is a fantasy.

"I see now that memory must be refuted on the same grounds as time. It is merely the reflection of a past that no longer exists, like light from a distant star that reaches us long after the star has been extinguished. It is an illusion."

Death was an illusion. Time was an illusion. Memory was an illusion. Was there anything that wasn't an illusion?

"I'll tell you something that's not an illusion," Dr. Marlow said, sidling up behind Borges. "Dinner. It's very real and it will be served in your room in five minutes."

That announcement triggered an unseemly rush by the patients—Patrick racing ahead, followed by Walter, who must have doubted that he could ever overtake him, melancholy

Ivan loping dejectedly behind—to lay aside all metaphysical doubts and adjourn to their room, nearly upsetting the cart laden with covered trays that was taking them their dinner. Sister Joseph pushed Alonso's wheelchair in the other direction, toward his room, and Father Geraghty drifted away in a muffled conversation with Dr. Marlow, leaving Borges and me in sole possession of the card table and the whisky bottle.

"Just as there are no atheists in foxholes," Borges said, "there are no amnesiacs at the dinner table. What man can forget his stomach?"

"Not this one," I said, eager to go home to dinner with my wife.

"Let's have another whisky before dinner."

I refilled our glasses and we settled back to enjoy our drinks. "It was my blindness that enabled me to understand the nature of memory, and of reality," Borges said.

I waited for him to go on.

"When I was forty years old," he continued, "the visible world began to recede from my consciousness. I became a stranger to the world of appearances, or at any rate a visitor, through the artifice of memory. My library and my eyesight had been my most prized possessions. I could not bear to lose both of them. So over a fifteen-year period I saved my library by memorizing it. To succeed at this required a mnemonic strategy. I studied the art of memory as taught by Simonides and used by our friend Ivan to entertain crowds in music halls and traveling circuses.

"As I memorized my library it dawned on me that writing itself is a mnemonic device, and reading is recollection. When you read, you see the arbitrary symbols we call letters, arranged in distinctive groups, and they make you remember a word. And I would go farther and say listening is recollection. The phonetic sounds of speech—the words themselves—are they not also a mnemonic device? And they exist to remind us of..."

His voice trailed off as he seemed to concentrate on his whisky, sipping it gingerly, savoring the taste, daubing his lips with his napkin—and leaving me in suspense as I waited for him to finish his sentence. What is the essence of things that language is a reminder of? What is the reality that stands behind our attempt to describe it with language?

If he sensed my eagerness for an answer, he dismissed it with a wave of the hand. "What do words exist to remind us of," he mused, echoing my thoughts, "but the fleeting, constantly-changing mental states which to each of us represent the world? Which *are* the world, according to Schopenhauer. Thus language itself is a mnemonic device. We use it to find our way through the labyrinth of our own minds."

"Of reality, I would have said."

"Ah, but they are the same thing."

Sister Joseph, appearing before us, insisted that Borges return to his room for dinner. I would come back the next day, I told him, calculating what it would cost me to miss another day of work. I assumed it would be another day of verbal legerdemain, playful paradoxes, and excruciating promenades. But a different sort of reality lay in wait for us, a reality that was not just of the mind. By two o'clock the next afternoon, one of the men who had just left the room would be dead.

"You think you know what you remember," Borges said as he rose to his feet. "Of course you do—that's what it means to know something. But how do you know that you know it? Is there anything you can check a memory against except another memory? How do you know that other memory is correct without checking it against some other one? And so on with that one and the next, *ad infinitum*. This—the vertigo of infinite regress—is why I have a horror of mirrors, even though I can't see them. The world cannot exist more than once without veering into unreality and terror."

I handed him his walking stick and we began the slow journey back to his room.

"My blindness has taught me all this and more," he said, "which to you, who live in the world of appearances, must remain a mystery."

4.

The next morning was cold and foggy, threatening rain. Unable to reach anyone at the university who claimed responsibility for Borges, I took the day off from work and braved the rush-hour traffic to drive to the hospital. Arriving at the Amnesia Ward, I found Borges, fully dressed in his dark suit and tie, his thin gray hair neatly combed back, sitting alone on one of the stuffed chairs in the lobby, as if waiting to be discharged. The only other patient in sight was Alonso Quijano, who slouched in his wheelchair a few feet from Borges, reciting a litany of diseases he claimed to suffer from, including scurvy, malaria and African sleeping sickness.

"At least there's one illness you don't have," Borges said. "Hypochondria."

"I thank God for sparing me that," Alonso laughed, twirling the tips of his Salvador Dalí mustache.

I cleared my throat to let them know I was there. "Are they letting you out?" I asked Borges.

"I'm afraid so. Dr. Marlow asked me to wait here. I will try to talk her into letting me stay."

I helped him adjust his clothes so he'd look his best for the doctor. From what he'd said, I knew he would use every trick in the book to stay in the hospital. And that book, like all of his books, would be a parcel of fantasies, paradoxes and deceptions. He was a kind of literary Munchausen, who could conjure up the most baffling conundrums if he thought people would fall for them.

After a moment Dr. Marlow came in and sat across from us. She wore a bright clean lab coat over a dark blue dress and held a pen and a small spiral notebook in her hands. "We need to evaluate your condition, Dr. Borges," she said.

"Of course."

"Do you mind having Nick here while we talk?"

"To   the   contrary"—he   raised   his   forefinger authoritatively—"I insist on having him here."

She glanced at Alonso, who, stricken with African sleeping sickness, sprawled in his wheelchair snoring like a buzz saw. "What about Mr. Quijano? Should I ask the nurse to take him back to his room?"

"Not at all. His bestiary of imaginary diseases reminds me how lucky I am to have only two or three of them. Talking about them may help me recover my memory."

"That's what I wanted to discuss with you," she said, setting the notebook on her lap so she could take notes. "When you came in after the accident you had what we call retrograde amnesia—it's a common effect of head trauma."

"Accident? I don't remember any accident."

Dr. Marlow took that objection in stride. "Yes, naturally your amnesia would include the events immediately before and after the trauma, as well as the trauma itself."

"There was no accident, no trauma. My amnesia, if you want to call it that, began many years ago. Indeed it spans my entire life."

"Dr. Borges." She was on the verge of exasperation. "The accident happened. You have a memory impairment."

"Nothing like Alonso's, at least. We were chatting before you got here. He remembers other people's memories."

"There's a name for that," the doctor said. "Aliomnemonism. The belief that your memories belong to someone else."

"In fact he believes that his are the memories of one person in particular: William Shakespeare."

She broke into a grin. "How does he say he acquired Shakespeare's memories?"

"He was sitting in a bar in Calcutta and a British expatriate by the name of Brixley offered to give him Shakespeare's memory. Not just the parts everyone knows but all the minor details as well. Rough drafts, lost plays, the identity of the dark lady—the works. He accepted the offer and gradually Shakespeare's memory planted itself in his mind. That's what he claims, but of course I don't believe him. I know he's crazy."

"The polite word—the medical word—is delusional."

"I confess I have a touch of the same delusion. I retain specific memories—what happened yesterday, ten years ago, sixty years ago—as well as anyone. But I can't remember *whom* those things happened to. To me or to someone else? It seems to me that I've spent my life as an impostor, pretending to be Borges."

"You're not Borges?"

"Only intermittently."

Clearly it was time for an intervention. "Borges has maintained as long as I've known him that he's an impostor," I explained to Dr. Marlow. "In the sense that everyone is an impostor, asserting a continuous personal identity that doesn't really exist. It's a philosophical stance, not an impairment."

Alonso, suddenly wide awake, sat up in his wheelchair and spoke out on the side of impostors. "I am not what I am," he declared.

"Well put, Alonso," Borges laughed. "Shakespeare couldn't have said it better."

The conversation continued in the same vein for several minutes, more resembling a dialogue from *Through the Looking-Glass* than your typical doctor-patient interaction. By the time it ended, Borges had qualified for another night in the Amnesia Ward. If he didn't tone it down, I wanted to warn him, he might win six months in a padded cell.

Then—I think it was about 11:00 o'clock—the elevator door opened and out trooped Patrick's visitors from the day before: his wife Lorraine, with her taut, thin-lipped face, her air of a jaded divorcee-in-waiting; his partner Brian Daley, with his showy informality, like an Elvis imitator in a blue leisure suit; the pothead son Andrew, and the cynical daughter Daphne, dressed all in black as if she was hoping for a funeral. They marched past Borges, who beamed back inscrutably as if he could see them, and on past Alonso, still muttering quotations from Shakespeare, until they came face to face with Dr. Marlow, who had risen to greet them. "I'm so glad you're here," she said. "Patrick made a major breakthrough this morning. His memory is coming back."

You might have thought they'd be overjoyed, or at least happy, or at least mildly interested. But their expressions were what you'd have expected if the doctor had handed them the bill. In that family the past was a mausoleum they preferred to keep under lock and key.

"That's wonderful," Lorraine said.

Here in the Memory Care Center, as I think back on that morning in the Amnesia Ward so long ago, I'm amazed that I can still remember anything about it. Right now my memory has a half-life of about thirty days. In that span of time I will lose half the memories I have now, then in the next thirty days, half of the remainder, and so on, like Walter's diminishing projections of my life expectancy, until—until what? What will my mind consist of when all those jagged puzzle-pieces of my soul have been scattered by time?

One thing I remember is what Borges said that day after the McColgan family went to the patients' room and Dr. Marlow padded away. He gripped my wrist with one hand and tapped his walking stick on the floor with the other, and we proceeded twice around the lobby and down the long hall to the room, at our barely perceptible pace, as he told me the story of an emptying mind. "I once knew—or possibly imagined—a young man who had an uncanny gift of recall," he said. "The boy remembered everything he saw down to the tiniest detail—each sunrise, each blade of grass, each leaf—then half of the leaf, a quarter of the leaf, and so on down to the tiniest subdivisions. So many unique memories crowded his mind that, like Ivan, he lost all practical use of his memory. Everything he remembered was so specific that he lost his ability to conceptualize and became incapable of reason. All too young, he sickened and died."

"What a shame," I said.

"To survive in the world you must perceive it in conceptual categories which you label with words and identify, incorrectly, as the world itself. Then in old age you find yourself groping for words and not finding them. First the nouns, then the adjectives, then the verbs and adverbs, all begin to vanish from your memory. And then, I presume, the concept represented by each word will vanish as well. What's left in your mind when all this is gone?"

"I don't know," I confessed, not realizing that he was describing the situation I'd find myself in fifty years later.

"If there's anything left after a word and the concept it represents are gone," he went on, "it must be the original experience or perception the word first stood for in your mind. You remember that perception, that experience, detached from language and its categories. And what does it mean to remember an experience in that way, without language? Isn't it to *repeat* the experience, to *relive* it? Otherwise it would be remembering the category, not the experience. If you can do that, even for one thing—if you can recapture the actual experience of something free of its category—we must count you enlightened, blessed even, a saint, a Zen master, adrift in a timeless moment plucked from eternity."

5.

The next three hours are a blur in my memory. Patrick entertained us with his oblivious high spirits, Walter with his idiot-savant predictions. Ivan never took his eyes off the clock, as if by fixing his mind on the seconds, minutes and hours ticking by he could negate Borges's refutation of time. Lorraine sniped at Daphne, Daphne sparred with Brian, Brian taunted Andrew, while Borges and Father Geraghty debated

St. Anselm's proof of the existence of God. The patients ate lunch while the rest of us cast ravenous glances at their food trays. Sister Joseph came in at 1:30 and said Patrick needed to take his nap. The rest of us, besides Borges, who also needed a nap, and Ivan, who couldn't tear his eyes away from the clock, were relocated to the lobby while Patrick slept. It was warm out there and I dozed off more than once. In my somnolent state I heard people arguing, laughing, coming and going, until the noise died down and all was quiet. When I opened my eyes I was alone in the lobby except for Daphne, who sat by herself flipping through the pages of *People* magazine.

And then came the anxious shouting, the hurried footsteps, the hushed phone calls. An emergency team raced through the ward and down the corridor to the room, where Borges clutched his walking stick, Ivan stared at the clock, and Patrick lay dead, his face purple, his tongue lolling out. He had been smothered with his pillow.

The lobby was thronged with security guards brandishing walkie-talkies and spools of yellow tape who quickly set about locking the ward down. They taped off the patients' room and took up positions blocking the elevators, the stairways, the emergency exits. No one was to touch anything or leave the ward until the police arrived.

The lobby was a scene of desperate consternation. Patrick's family, indifferent if not hostile to him in life, seemed devastated by his death, their mutual loathing apparently canceled by their grief. Everyone but Ivan— Daphne and Lorraine, Andrew and Brian, even Walter, who until a few minutes before had been such a staunch skeptic about death—stood hugging and sobbing and consoling each other with platitudes about the inexorability of fate and the transitoriness of human life. The nurses led Borges and Ivan out to the lobby, where I sat between them. "If Hell is other people," Borges whispered in my ear, "I think we've been sent where we belong."

Dr. Marlow stood by the nurses' station calling for our attention. "I'm sorry to have to keep you locked up like this," she said. "The police want everyone to come down to the common room for what I hope will be a brief meeting."

"Doctor," Borges spoke up unexpectedly. "Would you guide me down there? There's something I'd like to discuss with you." He pushed himself up with his walking stick and extended his arm. Dr. Marlow took it and the two of them began a slow journey to the common room, murmuring in conspiratorial tones. "Nick," Borges said, raising his voice, "you go ahead and save me a good seat in the front row. And please put Ivan in the seat next to mine."

I went ahead, escorting Ivan as he suggested. In the common room, which adjoined the lobby on the other side of the nurses' station, fifteen or twenty chairs had been arranged in rows, leaving a space in the front where three uniformed cops and a plainclothes detective waited for the invited guests. As he requested, I saved a seat for Borges in the front row and seated Ivan next to it. Since I wanted a better view of the proceedings than I could get there, I took a seat about three rows back, just behind Patrick's family. Brian parked himself between Lorraine and Daphne, with Andrew beside his sister. Walter settled in the second row, behind the seat I'd saved for Borges. When Dr. Marlow came in with Borges, she guided him to the empty chair in the front row and sat down beside Walter. Father Geraghty and Sister Joseph were already there, along with a dozen other nurses and patients. Even the Munchausen patient, Alonso Quijano, in the throes of myasthenia gravis or African sleeping sickness or some other delusional disease, had been wheeled into the back where he slouched with his head drooping over his chest.

I found it surprising that Borges had sent me ahead while he conferred with Dr. Marlow. What did the old conjurer have up his sleeve? Whatever it was, I was happy not to be part of it. I knew we were in for an entertaining spectacle when I recognized the plainclothes officer as Detective Ed Harrity, whom Borges and I had encountered in one of our early cases. That was five or six years before, and even then Harrity had seemed as beaten down as a cop could be without taking refuge behind a desk. Now he looked about sixty going on ninety-five. His furrowed complexion, his shopworn smile, his blue eyes faded to gray told the story of his life. It was an old story and a sad one. Thirty years on the force had hammered him into a hard-case archetype of the cynical cop.

He was not immune to all emotion, however. His lopsided face flushed with alarm at the sight of Borges in the front row. "Hey, don't I know you from somewhere?"

"The DeMarce case," Borges nodded with obvious pride. It had been Borges, after all, who solved that case, knocking out the perpetrator with one brutal swipe of his walking stick while Harrity stood helpless on the sidelines. For Harrity that must have been the low point in an undistinguished career. He jerked his thumb toward the elevators. "You're free to go."

"I'm not going anywhere," Borges said. "I am an eyewitness to the crime and thus essential to its solution."

"A blind eyewitness?" Harrity scoffed.

"In the land of the one-eyed, the blind man is king."

"Dr. Borges needs to stay," Dr. Marlow said. "He was in the room when Mr. McColgan died."

"Then I'm warning you, Dr. Borges," the detective grimaced, "if you're really a doctor—"

"Doctor of Literature, University of Cuyo, 1956." Borges inclined his head in a modest bow. "Honorary."

"You have the right to remain silent, and that's what you damn well better do. One peep and I'll haul you in for interference. And keep your mitts off that cane."

Detective Harrity's truculence melted into weary scorn as he peered out over the crowd. It was the kind of scene Borges regarded as ideal at the climax of an investigation, with all the principals in one room to hear the detective announce his solution to the crime. The only trouble—and I could see it coming as soon as Borges parked himself in the front row—was that the investigation had barely begun and Harrity, not Borges, was the detective. How long, I wondered, would he remain in control of the investigation?

The policeman cleared his throat to command the crowd's attention. "I've asked you all to stay here while the coroner makes his preliminary determination whether Mr. McColgan was murdered or died from natural causes. If it was murder—"

"I beg your pardon, Detective," Borges interrupted. "There can be no doubt that it was murder. It was the second attempt on the man's life within a week."

"The first time was attempted suicide."

"Nonsense," Borges scoffed, and he proceeded to demonstrate, as he had done for us the night before, that beyond question, given the trajectory of the bullet, Patrick McColgan had been shot by someone who overpowered him in his office.

Harrity ignored Borges and tried to regain control. "As I mentioned," he said, "the coroner will rule on whether this death was from natural causes or not. If it was murder, you should all consider yourselves suspects. You're under no obligation to speak, but anything you say may be used against you."

"You're very much mistaken if you think all the people in this room could be suspects," Borges interjected. "Haven't you ever read a detective story? A murder can't have more than six potential suspects."

"You think this is some kind of fantasy we're talking about?"

"Not at all. But do you suppose that the conventions of literature have no relevance to a criminal investigation? That would be like saying epic poetry has no application to military strategy."

It was one of Borges's pet ideas. He believed—or pretended to believe, if it would exasperate an adversary— that reality shapes itself according to the same archetypes as literature, and that any apparent distinction between literature and reality is illusory and unworthy of serious consideration.

Harrity laughed nervously and appealed to Dr. Marlow. "Are you sure this isn't the psych ward?"

The doctor was not amused. "I'd appreciate if you'd stick to police business and leave the medical judgments to us. These patients are here to be respected, not ridiculed."

"I apologize," Harrity grunted. "I'm doing the best I can, what with all the interruptions."

"You should try listening to what the patients have to say. Maybe you'll learn something."

Beads of sweat glistened on the detective's forehead. He took a deep breath and daubed at them with a handkerchief. "I hate to admit it," he said, eyeing Borges, "but you make a valid point. Not everybody here is a suspect. Your disability rules you out. The same thing applies to the gentleman in the wheelchair."

"I think we can safely rule out all the patients," Dr. Marlow said. "What conceivable motive could they have had?"

"I wouldn't rule myself out," Walter piped up, peeking out from under his beetling brows. "Speaking as an actuary, of course."

That was almost too much for Harrity. "You mind telling me what the hell that means?"

"Actuarial science predicts the future with a high degree of accuracy by focusing on the aggregate, not the individual. If an actuary predicts that 147 white males will die in Boston this week, that's exactly what will happen, regardless of what any individual does or doesn't do. One of those men might very well get smothered with a pillow."

"Kismet," the detective muttered derisively.

Walter pushed his glasses up his nose and waited for them to slide back down. "Something like that."

"Did you have any reason to kill Patrick McColgan?"

"No, but individual motive is irrelevant. If his time had come, and I happened to be there—"

"Let's stick with facts," Harrity growled. "Did you kill McColgan?"

Walter seemed embarrassed that fate had overlooked him. "Not that I recall, but—"

"Don't you think you'd remember if you killed him?"

"This is the Amnesia Ward," Dr. Marlow cut in. "You seem to have a lot of trouble remembering that."

6.

"Detective Harrity," Borges spoke up. "If I may."

"You may not," Harrity said through clenched teeth.

"You can't very well forbid me to speak if you don't know what I'm going to say. How do you know I'm not about to reveal the solution to the crime?"

The detective was foiled again. "Okay. Go on."

"Dr. Marlow is correct in focusing on motive," Borges said. "We all know a murder must have a motive. In fact, since the two attacks are connected, we know the motive for the second attack: it was to protect the identity of the assailant in the first attack. Mr. McColgan's memories were coming back, we'd been told. The assailant had to strike quickly to keep from being identified. So the question is, what was the motive for the first attack?"

"We've thought of that," Harrity said. "I've got a man down there right now—"

"The first assailant can't have been Ivan or Walter or Nick Martin or me or even Father Geraghty (much as I hate to admit it), because at that time Mr. McColgan had never met them. Walter says most murder victims know their killers; in this case it is a certainty. And it happens that we are sitting here with the handful of people Patrick knew best."

All eyes were on Lorraine, Daphne, Andrew, and Brian Daley, who writhed in their seats and shot accusatory glances around the room. They were like a bunch of snakes in the bottom of a bucket. You didn't know whether they'd slither away or swallow each other whole.

"The question is: Which one of them killed him?"

"You should be staring at Walter," Brian said, his eyes blazing. "He practically begged to be treated as a suspect and his motive is clear enough. He sees himself as an instrument of fate."

"To the contrary," Borges said, "he uses his actuarial skills to predict the workings of fate, not to direct them. In any case we know he could not have committed the murder.

One of the iron-clad rules of detection is that the murderer can't be a stranger who comes out of the woodwork to commit the crime. He (or she) must have appeared early in the case in a significant role. Now at the time of the first attack on Mr. McColgan, we must assume that Walter and Patrick had yet to meet."

"You have no evidence for that assumption."

"To assume the opposite would be preposterous."

"And no proof. You're angling at Lorraine and me but you have no proof that either of us killed Patrick or tried to kill him." As soon as Brian said that he must have known it was a blunder. The murderer is always the first to say the detective has no proof.

Borges let that *faux pas* pass without comment. "The proof will come later," he said. "First let's complete our analysis. If we eliminate Walter and Father Geraghty as suspects—"

"Why eliminate Father Geraghty?" Brian demanded. "He was in the room and left around the same time we did."

"Can I believe my ears?" Father Geraghty gasped. "Am I being accused of a mortal sin? A man of the cloth?"

"I've seen *The Exorcist,*" Brian said. "I've seen that girl's head spinning around. If a priest could do that—"

"Please!" Borges raised his hand to quell the argument. "A supernatural element in a murder investigation is always a red herring. Even if Father Geraghty could conjure demonic powers to smother Mr. McColgan with his pillow—a question on which I express no opinion—we cannot accept it as a solution to the mystery."

"Thank you," the priest nodded, still glowering at Brian. "So let's move on."

Borges had done a masterful job of focusing suspicion on Brian and Lorraine, and Brian had done a masterful job of incriminating himself. Now it was Lorraine's turn. "I'm not going to listen to this any longer!" she shrieked, lurching to her feet. She glared at Borges, then at Harrity. "Who is this Dr. Borges, anyway? He's no doctor. He's not even a policeman. He's a fake, a charlatan."

"Never underestimate the power of a charlatan," Borges said. "Facts and logic are correct even when asserted by a liar."

The same argument could have been made by the suspects. Those closest to Patrick—his family and his business partner—were certainly a deplorable lot, about as likeable as a swarm of hornets. But did that mean they were murderers?

Patrick's daughter Daphne chose that moment to join the fray. "Don't you think the first thing a detective ought to ask," she said, smirking at her stepmother, "is who's been sleeping with who?"

"Whom," Borges said. "Who's been sleeping with *whom.*"

"Whatever."

Lorraine took the insinuation in stride. "Well, Patrick's dead and we're going to get married so I guess there's no point in hiding it." She picked up Brian's hand and clutched it in her icy grip. "Yes, we've been in a relationship for over a year, and so has Patrick."

"Patrick? With whom?"

"His all-purpose secretary—Jane, I think her name is—whom he shared with Brian." Lorraine's eyebrows rose as she said "shared" and even Borges caught the implication.

"You shared her?"

Brian scowled and pulled his hand away. "As a secretary, yes. But no, I've never slept with her except in Lorraine's imagination."

"So this... accusation, is nothing new?" Borges asked.

"No, Lorraine's had this idea in her head for about six months."

"She thinks you were both cheating on her with the same woman? Astonishing!"

"Jane is a very attractive lady," Brian explained. "She's an actress, just does secretarial work to pay the rent. Any number of men—"

"She's basically a whore," Lorraine snarled.

"You've met her, then?"

"Of course I've met her. Every time I go to the office she's there draping herself around either Patrick or Brian, or both. And when I'm not looking, sleeping with both of them."

There was a long moment of silence, like the lull in an artillery barrage. Lorraine gazed over the battlefield at Brian, who looked like he wished he could crawl into a trench. Daphne smirked with delight at the firestorm she'd set off. Borges appeared—for the first time since I'd known him—at a loss for words. In the hands of an angry woman he quickly turned into something resembling putty, or perhaps overcooked spaghetti. "Well," he ventured, "I can see why you're so disturbed by this, but—"

"I'm not the least bit disturbed," Lorraine snapped. "I'm not the jealous type."

"No, of course not."

"I know how men are." That was her final judgment from which there could be no appeal.

"Obviously we shouldn't have hired Jane," Brian admitted. "A blond bombshell like that. I was against it but Patrick insisted. I think he had it in mind to take her to bed before the interview was over."

"Is she married?"

"Oh, yes. Her husband's another actor, but he doesn't work a second job so they're always strapped for cash. After Patrick started sleeping with her she barely did any work and I wanted to fire her, but he said no, she really needed the money. So we were basically paying her to have sex with Patrick. You can imagine how I felt about that."

"Quite angry, I would suppose."

Brian realized he'd compromised himself. "Well... sort of annoyed. And then the husband started calling the office and harassing me—he thought the same as Lorraine, that both of us were sleeping with her. Talk about jealous! Jane would get on the phone and make fun of him, called him Hamlet, Macbeth, Othello—whatever role he happened to be playing. Then one day she just quit without giving notice. I figured she and Patrick had a falling out, but no, he was still sleeping with her. I'd hear him in his office sweet talking her on the phone."

"Talk about jealous!" Lorraine said, her eyes dancing in triumph.

"Are you married?" Borges asked Brian.

"Sure. Debbie and I have been married for twenty years."

"Does she know about all this?"

"I told you I wasn't sleeping with Jane. There's nothing to know about."

"What about Lorraine? Does she know about Lorraine?"

His face fell. "No, she doesn't know about that. Are you crazy?"

"She will soon enough," Lorraine smiled. "When you tell her you're divorcing her."

"OK," Daphne said, trying to end the squabbling. "So there's this jealousy that my dad's having sex with Jane and you're paying for it. You're pissed, we all get that. But if you killed him—"

"I didn't kill him."

"But if you did, you must have had a stronger motive, right? Like the insurance money?"

"Insurance money?" Walter gasped. "That would clinch it. 98.6 percent of the time."

"Is there insurance money?" Borges asked.

Brian twisted his head from side to side as if he were trying to slip it out of a noose. "You might as well tell him," Lorraine said. "It's going to come out."

"OK, there's the key-man insurance," he said. "It's a kind of life insurance that business partners have. If either partner dies, the other one gets enough money to buy his share of the business from the heirs."

"So after Patrick's death you can exercise that and be the sole owner of the business? And the money goes to Lorraine?"

"That's right."

"And how much is that?"

"A couple million."

That lofty figure took a moment to sift and settle through the crowd. There were gasps and whistles and sighs and even a few ominous growls. Borges held his peace, as if lost in thought.

"I'll take it from here," Harrity said, stepping in front of him. He turned to Brian: "Is there anyone else who would benefit from that insurance besides you and Lorraine?"

The question kindled renewed hostility from Brian. "Well, since you're throwing accusations around: my wife Debbie would benefit. If we get divorced"—he ventured a glance into Lorraine's steely eyes—*"when* we get divorced, she'll get twice as much as she would have gotten if Patrick were still alive."

"And Debbie's not just the jealous type," Lorraine said. "She's the type who might actually kill somebody, especially Patrick. She loathed Patrick."

"Let's keep our eye on the ball," Harrity said. "The murder happened here. Is there any reason to believe Debbie ever came to the hospital?"

There was not, or so it seemed—no one spoke up, which brought an end to that line of inquiry. But just as Harrity opened his mouth to proceed, Sister Joseph raised her hand

and caught his attention with characteristic modesty. "Detective?"

"Yes, sister?" Harrity asked.

"Maybe she's the mystery woman."

"The mystery woman?"

"There's a woman who's been coming to visit Mr. McColgan every night since he's been in the hospital. Down in the post-surgical unit, until two nights ago when he was transferred up here. The nurses on the night shift down there told me about her. She always came by herself and they thought she was his wife. She only came at night."

"When was he transferred to the Amnesia Ward?"

"The night before last."

"And nobody's seen her since?"

"No, sir."

"What is that crazy wife of yours up to?" Lorraine asked Brian.

Brian blinked, shook his head. "Trust me, I have no idea."

A uniformed cop had entered the room from the hallway in the back. He signaled to Detective Harrity and motioned him forward. The cop handed Harrity a piece of paper and the two had a whispered conversation. Harrity motioned to another officer who stood in the back, and when he turned around he had his eyes on Brian. "Well, Mr. Daley, you've tried to pin the blame on everybody but yourself. On Walter and Father Geraghty and now even on your wife. You've even tried the 'you have no proof' argument."

"Well, you don't, do you?" Brian said.

Harrity took his time answering as he rolled his triumphant eyes across the crowd. "I didn't until I received this." He stuck the paper in front of Brian's face and waited for his reaction.

"What the hell is this?"

"It's the purchase receipt for the gun that Patrick McColgan was shot with. We just found it in your desk drawer at the office. And it's in your name."

Brian buried his face in his hands. Lorraine stared at her shoes.

Daphne laughed hysterically. "You hear that?" she cried. "They did it! Her and Brian. First they shot him and when that didn't work they followed him in here and smothered him with a pillow. You had to wonder why they were visiting so often."

With a nod to the uniformed cops, Detective Harrity glided up behind Brian and snapped handcuffs on his wrists. "Brian Daley," he intoned, "you are under arrest for the murder of Patrick McColgan. You have the right to remain silent. Anything you say may be held against you in a court of law."

7.

For one magical moment it seemed that the drama had played itself out. Once again the ideal of swift and certain justice had prevailed. The culprit had been apprehended and all that remained was for him to be tried by a jury of his peers.

But the illusion was shattered when Borges's hand shot up. "One moment, Detective!"

"You keep quiet or I'll put you in cuffs too."

"But I feel that I have no right to remain silent under the circumstances," Borges said.

"What are you talking about?"

"I know that Brian Daley is not the murderer."

"You're damn right I'm not the murderer," Brian growled.

"That bitch did it!" Lorraine screeched, lurching toward Daphne with her fists flying.

"You're calling *me* a bitch?" Daphne lashed out at Lorraine with her clawlike nails. "You murdered my dad!"

One of the cops threw himself between the two women and handcuffed them together back to back.

"Get your hands off her!" Andrew shouted, trying to tear Daphne away. He too ended up in cuffs, locked face to face with his beloved sister.

Four sets of handcuffs and two hefty cops were no match for the McColgan family. To the delight of Father Geraghty, they excoriated each other in a barrage of name-calling, accusations and threats of violence seldom matched in the modern world outside a maximum security prison. It was as if we'd been transported back to the seventeenth century with a full cast of depraved, hysterical and vengeful characters acting out the last scene in a Jacobean tragedy.

"No, no, no," Borges chuckled. "You're all quite mistaken."

The pandemonium abated momentarily while the McColgans paused to catch their breath. "Then who do you think the murderer is?" Harrity asked warily.

Borges ignored him and addressed the family. "I'm sure your hatred for each other is completely justified," he said, "and under ordinary circumstances you'd be quite right to tear each other limb from limb. But in the present case you must reconcile yourselves to the fact that Mr. McColgan was murdered by someone outside the family."

"Who was it?" Harrity demanded.

"Before I answer that, we need to identify one more link in the chain. I have a question for Sister Joseph. This mystery woman you mentioned. What does she look like?"

"The nurses described her as tall and blond, in her early thirties, and..." The nurse hesitated and lowered her eyes.

"Lives hang in the balance," Borges said. "You must overcome your modesty and speak forthrightly. Isn't that so, Father Geraghty?"

"Absolutely!" The priest seemed keen—almost too keen—to hear what the nun would say.

"Well," Sister Joseph went on, blushing deeply, "they said she... had a very well developed bosom."

"Oh, my God!" Brian blurted. "That must be Jane!"

"The secretary," Borges said. "I'm sure that's who it is."

"Did she have a key to the office?" Harrity asked Brian.

"Sure, when she worked there. And she could have made a copy before she turned it in."

"She shot Patrick," Lorraine said, pleading for Brian, "and since then she's come to the hospital every night, waiting for a chance to finish him off. And this afternoon she snuck into his room and smothered him with his pillow."

Harrity took down Jane's full name and address and sent the two officers to find her and take her to the station for questioning.

"Obviously Jane is the mystery woman," Borges said when they had left. "But it's equally obvious that she didn't kill Patrick McColgan. Indeed she loved him and that's why she visited every night. And if I may venture a guess, the reason she did that was to warn him that another attempt would be made on his life. Unfortunately those warnings fell, if not exactly on deaf ears, on a non-retentive mind."

"But if she knew somebody was going to kill him," Harrity objected, "why didn't she go to the police?"

"Because she was also trying to protect the murderer."

"What?"

"Who, I believe, was her husband."

"Oh my God!" Brian said.

"Yes, the madly jealous husband—Othello, she called him—who harassed you and Patrick on the phone, forced her to quit her job, and eventually let himself into the office with her key and shot Patrick and left him for dead."

"And stashed the receipt for the gun in my desk drawer!"

"Yes. If Patrick's death was ruled a suicide, the receipt would be irrelevant. But if foul play was suspected, the police would search the office (as they just have done) and tag you as the murderer."

"Do you hear that, Detective?" Brian shouted. "You can take these handcuffs off me now."

But Detective Harrity, having snared his prey, was not about to let him escape so easily. His weary eyes gleamed with a desperate determination to win this battle, if not against the culprit, then at least against Borges. "The problem with your latest fantasy," he growled, addressing Borges instead of Brian, "is where the hell is the husband? Nobody's ever laid eyes on him around here. Whoever killed McColgan went into his room when everyone was napping and suffocated him—you think the secretary's husband did that?"

"Correction," Borges said. "Not everyone was napping. In fact the family and Brian and Walter were not even in the room. The only ones in that room, besides Patrick, were Ivan and me."

"And I suppose you were wide awake?"

"I rarely sleep."

"And now you're about to tell us you witnessed the murder?"

Borges let the question linger in the air while he daubed his forehead with a handkerchief. "I did indeed," he said. "I was an eyewitness, a blind eyewitness as you said earlier. My perception of events does not come to me through vision, but through hearing and thought and memory. This is how I witnessed the murder: I heard the sound of a struggle in the direction of Patrick's bed. I raised my head and aimed my sightless eyes toward that sound for thirty or forty seconds."

"Some eyewitness!" Harrity scoffed.

"The murderer must have known that I was blind, or I would have been smothered along with Patrick—for the same reason, to shut me up. So there's something a blind eyewitness can tell you that a sighted one couldn't have done: the murderer wasn't some stranger, some mystery man or woman wandering around the hospital. He—or she—had been here in the Amnesia Ward all along."

"Wait a minute! Who was there in the room with you?"

"Only Ivan, as I've said. When I heard the first sounds of struggle, I called out to him and he made no response. I know he was awake because I'd heard him clearing his throat just moments before. When he sleeps he stops clearing his throat and snores."

A breathless silence gripped the room as everyone waited for the big reveal. Was Ivan the murderer? Was he Jane's husband (who we'd learned was an actor and thus probably a gifted dissembler)? Had he been faking all along?

Borges took his time; he knew how to play a crowd. "I hate to disappoint you," he said after a long pause, "at least those of you who can't bear any more suspense, and those of you who are rooting for Brian Daley and the McColgan family to be released from captivity. But I must tell you forthrightly that Ivan was not the murderer. He was an eyewitness just as I was, but his vision, unlike mine, is unimpaired. The murderer, having observed him, assumed that he had no memory, just as I had no eyesight, and therefore wouldn't be able to help solve the crime. Ivan is the one you ought to be questioning."

Detective Harrity suppressed a smile. "Isn't he another amnesia case?"

"Ivan is tormented by a memory disorder," Borges said, "which, as I understand it, is the opposite of amnesia. It makes him aware of so many details and ramifications of his perceptions that he can't process or recall them. Is that correct, Dr. Marlow?"

"That's substantially correct," the doctor agreed.

"I believe he witnessed the murder without knowing it— or remembering it, which amounts to the same thing. You could question him about it, Detective, but I must warn you, such questioning could take a long time—"

"I have all day," Harrity said.

"Possibly an infinite amount of time, since his mind subdivides each memory into endlessly smaller segments, which in turn subdivide *ad infinitum,* much like Achilles's arrow in Zeno's paradox. You can't pull him out of that labyrinth just by asking a sequence of questions. But perhaps we can help him find his way by giving him a clue that he can follow out to daylight. Dr. Marlow, you'll recall that the mnemonic technique he used as a professional mnemonist— the method of Simonides—involved associating each memory with some object or symbol that was already in his mind."

"Yes, that's correct."

Borges shifted in his seat and cast his ethereal gaze in Ivan's direction. "Ivan," he said in the soothing voice of a hypnotist, "I want to guide you into your memory. I promise not to take you farther than you want to go."

Ivan stared blankly ahead as if Borges were talking to someone else. "It's okay, Ivan," Dr. Marlow said. "I'm right here."

"Ivan," Borges said, "imagine that you're in our room here in the Amnesia Ward. It's afternoon nap time but you're unable to sleep. As usual your eyes are on the wall clock, watching the second hand spin around, but you become aware of something else going on in the room. Someone is standing over Patrick's bed, leaning over him with a pillow, pressing it down on his face."

Ivan started to mutter. "White," he said. "Flowers, petals, red, wooden, lamp, cup, plastic, water..."

"Is that the side table you're describing? What's going on in the bed?"

"Kicking, arms swinging, fighting, choking, breathing..."

"Yes, that's what's happening to Patrick. Now who's doing it? Is it a man?"

"Leaning, pushing, shadows, white, pajamas..."

"Pajamas? Is he a patient?"

"Hands, fingers, hair, arms, mustache, wheelchair..."

"Wheelchair?"

There followed a collective gasp and a desperate turning of heads—not least of all Detective Harrity's, which may have spun all the way around like the girl's in *The Exorcist*—toward the back of the room, where Alonso Quijano had last been seen in his wheelchair. Needless to say, that gentleman was nowhere in evidence.

Borges beamed triumphantly. "We have identified the jealous husband, and the murderer of Patrick McColgan. He is that fantastical man in the wheelchair who calls himself Alonso Quijano Not his real name, of course—he is a master of many roles who has undoubtedly slipped away beyond the reach of the law."

Harrity waved to one of the cops, who rushed into the hallway. "He won't get far in that wheelchair."

"Of course he will," Borges said. "The wheelchair is a ruse which has fooled you all."

The old bard was in his glory. "I am told that the man is a Munchausen, a kind of madman who feigns illness. He assumed the name Alonso Quijano—the given name of Don Quixote de la Mancha (that alone should have tipped you off, Detective Harrity), who was also a madman, though in this case the madman made everyone believe he was only simulating madness, not unlike Hamlet, another avenger who plotted murder with madness as his disguise. It took a blind man to see through it."

"But who is he?" Lorraine demanded.

"He is the man your husband cuckolded. I don't know his name."

"Sidney Pockett," Brian said. "His name is Sidney Pockett."

The madman Sidney Pockett a/k/a Alonso Quijano was picked up the next morning wandering along Memorial Drive. He denied all recollection of who he was and where he'd been and was committed to the state mental hospital, from which he later escaped by impersonating a psychiatrist. His whereabouts remained a mystery until the mid-1990s, when he was discovered practicing holistic medicine in Keene, New Hampshire. Walter recovered enough of his memory to amass a considerable fortune as a professional poker player. His life expectancy is 8.3 years and growing. Mercifully I have forgotten what became of Brian Daley and the McColgans. All I remember is that Detective Harrity—it turned out there was some good in him after all—kept them handcuffed together for the next several hours as they polished their repertoire of mutual fear and loathing. Through each other they had found their own private Hell.

The case of Ivan became the subject of an important paper by Dr. Marlow, published in the *International Review of Neurology* the following year. Taking her cue from Borges (without attribution), Dr. Marlow wrote that Ivan suffered from an excess of memory, not a deficit. It recorded his perceptions by parsing each moment into the same infinitesimal subdivisions that stopped Achilles's arrow in midflight, thus paralyzing his memory. Through hypnosis, Dr. Marlow succeeded in extricating him from this labyrinth when she discovered that his amnesia resulted from a traumatic event that occurred during a wartime performance which had worked its way into the framework he used to evoke other memories.

Borges scoffed when I told him about the article. "Hypnosis belongs in the same category as exorcism, voodoo, and psychoanalysis," he said. "Pure quackery. I can only be thankful I never fell into the clutches of this Dr. Marlow."

"But you were under her care for several days!" I protested. "Don't you remember? You were in the Amnesia Ward at St. Aloysius, in a room with three other men, one of whom was murdered by his girlfriend's jealous husband while you were there."

"Murdered? A man in my room was murdered?"

"Smothered with his pillow while you lay awake on the next bed."

"Do you expect me to believe such a preposterous tale? What is this, the *Arabian Nights?*"

"Maybe you've forgotten."

"No," he declared with a definitive wag of the forefinger. "I don't remember forgetting that."

∞

Living in the Memory Care Center is like being stranded on a desert island. My two daughters—I love them both dearly—are my only visitors. Ingrid is the incarnation of everything a misanthrope would try to instill in a child. She's joyless, humorless, hard-working, an unwelcome conscience flushing out my weaknesses with inquisitorial zeal. Her younger sister Gracie is the soul I've always longed for but could never find in myself—the grasshopper to Ingrid's ant: funny, tolerant, talkative, happily indifferent to the troubles of the world. Gracie would gladly see my memories drain away if that would make me happy; Ingrid's chief concern is that I not be allowed to forget my regrets. The two of them are the only visitors to my desert island because everybody else wants to forget me before I forget them.

When the doctor diagnosed my condition I didn't believe him. Gracie indulged me in my denial, but Ingrid kept a sharp eye out for lapses of memory and attention that would confirm the worst. Secretly I mimicked her scrutiny, like a Puritan searching his predestined soul for evidence of damnation. When it turned out that the doctor was right, I was angrier than I'd ever been before. For a long time I resisted moving to the Memory Care Center. I would argue endlessly with Ingrid and the doctor, but the more I argued, the more demented I seemed. Finally even Gracie took their side and I had no choice but to surrender.

Here the routine can be mind-numbing. The memory police make their rounds, badgering me with intimidating questions at any hour of the day or night. I do not have the right to remain silent, and every lapse or hesitation will be used against me. I've never told them about the real memory work I'm doing: searching through lost time for those priceless hours I spent with Borges and trying at last to understand them. When I dive down into those regions, there's always something that rears up and blocks my view, and it's always the same thing, the biggest regret of my life— the accident that took Katie from me. The blinding lights, the squealing tires, the slow-motion vertigo of the inevitable. The agony of my twisted back, the eerie detachment of Katie in her coma, and then her disappearance from the world. I've tried to consign it all to oblivion, imagining vainly that forgetting is a voluntary act. But the back pain which has tortured me since the accident is my *petite madeleine,* the small fragment of the past that keeps bringing it all back to the surface.

My best friend here is Timothy, a retired tire salesman with bristling white eyebrows, a lopsided mouth, and a vast blotchy forehead like a map of the moon. I enjoy talking to Timothy because he doesn't remember a word I say. One afternoon I told him about Katie and the torment she endured when the girls were teenagers. Ingrid was domineering, unpopular, mad at the world; Gracie wild, a free spirit, indomitable. They had always been close, and in those years their closeness became volatile. Katie struggled to hold them together while keeping them apart. The day arrived when they nearly came to blows. On whatever provocation, Gracie dragged Ingrid down the stairs and threw her out into the cold, locking the door behind her. I came home from work and found them sullen and unforgiving, Katie in tears.

As I told this story to Timothy, Ingrid and Gracie arrived for their weekly visit, gliding in unnoticed behind me. Timothy, sphinxlike in his wheelchair, paid them no mind.

"You don't remember that," Ingrid said, her voice whining like a saw blade.

"Of course I do." I turned to face her. She's as beautiful as her mother was, without the least resemblance. Her eyes gleamed back at me like raven's wings.

"I can't believe you're going around making up lies behind my back."

Gracie kept her own counsel, feigning a memory lapse. I recalled the incident quite clearly. For two weeks the two of them didn't acknowledge each other's existence. It was as if only their ghosts lived in the house. Then somehow they reached a truce—in fact they needed each other. After that they were closer than ever, each more wary, yet more assured of her place in the world.

"His memory disorder includes remembering a lot of things that never happened," Ingrid told Timothy, evidently mistaking his mindlessness for rapt attention. "You can disregard anything he says about us."

"I'm sure he will," I said.

She changed the subject to something less personal. "Has he told you about Borges?" she asked Timothy, again eliciting no response.

"Borges was real," I said. "Have you tried looking him up?"

"There was a real Borges," she conceded. "I've read two biographies that never mentioned you or any of the things he supposedly did with you."

"That's to be expected. I've told you about his claim to be an impostor. When he was with me he was traveling incognito."

"The man in those biographies was the real Borges," she said. "The one you talk about existed only in your imagination. What you think you remember are your own fantasies."

I wouldn't have admitted it to Ingrid, but her accusation was difficult to refute. When you look into your mind, how can you tell the difference between the actual past and an imagined one? But I might have argued, if I'd been spoiling for a fight, that our experience of the present is no less a fantasy. What is the present but the fleeting boundary between the past, which no longer exists, and the future, which has yet to exist? It's a particle of time which lacks the defining characteristic of time, which is duration. How can we experience the present unless it exists for some length of time? And if we can't experience it, our knowledge and recollection of it can only be a fantasy.

Borges maintained that memory is the key to all understanding, that without memory the universe cannot exist—*does* not exist, in fact.

More than a year after his stay in the Amnesia Ward, we were driving up to New Hampshire to attend a seminar on Nordic mythology at a remote north woods conference retreat. A cloudy day in early November, as I recall, the landscape vast and gray as a northern sea. For the first hour he sat motionless in the passenger seat without saying a word, and then suddenly, as if picking up the thread of an interrupted conversation, he began to talk. "I mentioned Bishop Berkeley when I said time is an illusion," he said. "Berkeley said we know only our perceptions of the world and not the world itself. From that observation he concluded that the physical world exists only to the extent that it is perceived. *Esse est percipi*—to exist is to be perceived—is how he put it."

The idea sounded vaguely familiar. I think he'd mentioned it more than once before.

"But I would go farther—you'll excuse me, I hope, if this sounds like the special pleading of a blind man—and say that perception itself cannot account for existence. The mind is not a polished slate that passively receives perceptions without selecting them, altering them, classifying them, all of which take time and therefore require memory."

"You're saying you need your memory just to perceive things?"

"Nothing we perceive enters or stays in our minds except to the extent that we remember it. Thus I would say, not *esse est percipi,* but *esse est memoria*: to exist is to be remembered. The physical world exists not in the perceiving mind but in the remembering mind."

At the time, I'll admit, I'd never given a thought to *where* the physical world exists. It just exists, doesn't it? Even if, as we're told, 99.99% of the universe is empty space, including the space between the atoms and between the tiny particles that make up the atoms. The other 0.01%, the part that isn't empty space, obviously exists right where it is. Or so it seemed to me at the time.

"Memory," Borges went on, "though to us it seems as obvious as the axioms of arithmetic, exists as a contingent fact of nature: it could be otherwise. The ability to hold a thought or a fact in our minds for a certain length of time defines us as humans. If it were much shorter, there would be no language, no culture, no religion, no science; if it were much longer, we might fancy ourselves gods. In either case we would be an altogether different kind of creature—and we would live in an entirely different universe."

As things turned out, we never made it to the Nordic mythology seminar. But for the next few days, the nature of the physical universe—where it exists, how it exists, even *whether* it exists when nobody's watching—would be very much on our minds, as recorded in my second story, entitled "The Ninth Life of Schrödinger's Cat."

The Ninth Life of Schrödinger's Cat

I think I can safely say that nobody
understands quantum mechanics.

— Richard Feynman

The call came the day after Halloween. Borges had arrived
from Buenos Aires and checked into the Copley Plaza Hotel,
expecting to be greeted and guided by an Argentine scholar at
Harvard named Juan Murchison. The plan was for Murchison
to drive him to and from the Nordic mythology conference
in New Hampshire, entertain him at Harvard for a few days,
and then put him on a plane back to Argentina. But
Murchison had taken ill and no one at Harvard could spare
the time to substitute for him. Naturally Borges called me,
who always seemed to be available for duty as a sidekick,
driver, and major domo. I had the added advantage of having
assisted in his exploits as a detective, in the unlikely event that
any detecting needed to be done. I'd reached the point in my
job where I needed a few days off, so against my better
judgment I said yes. In the past few weeks I hadn't been an
easy person to get along with and Katie was probably glad to
see me go.

We drove north through the drizzle along two-lane roads, then one-lane roads and finally dirt tracks that wound through an endless forest of pines and hemlocks, the trees taller and darker, the shadows deeper and more forbidding with each passing mile. It was an ideal locale for a seminar on Nordic mythology, with its malign spirits, bloody horrors and savage attacks by wild beasts. I checked my gas gauge as a gray wraith of a town emerged from the mist and quickly vanished behind us. I caught a glimpse of one ramshackle filling station but saw no place to eat or sleep. Fortunately, as Borges had assured me, we'd be dining and sleeping at the conference center.

It was dusk by the time we arrived, and the place looked all but deserted. There was a low-roofed main lodge surrounded by a ring of wooden cabins nestled among the towering pines. A scattering of cars was parked along the road and in front of the cabins. Borges insisted on getting out of the car with me, and we proceeded, at a glacial pace—his walking stick in one hand, my elbow in the other—toward the entrance to the main lodge, where some lights could be seen inside.

A tall, striking woman leaned in the doorway languidly smoking a cigarette. She greeted us with a welcoming but skeptical smile, as if she could tell at a glance that we didn't belong there.

"We're here for the mythology conference," I told her.

"Oh, dear!" she said. "That's not until next week."

"What's going on, then?"

"Theoretical physics. We'll be here till Friday."

So there we were. Tired and hungry at a rustic camp in the middle of the woods, stumbling into the funhouse mirror of theoretical physics, where nothing is what it seems. It was cold and almost dark and we had no place to stay for the night.

The woman held out a graceful hand. "I'm Francine Morrison," she said, widening her smile. "You need to talk to my husband. He's the director."

She led us inside where Bob Morrison stood chatting with a pair of younger men. Tall, tan and silver-haired, he was well known, I later learned, for the brilliance of his early work on quantum mechanics with Feynman at Cornell. Now he was a popular professor at MIT, often consulted by the government and a regular on the conference circuit. At sixty, he exuded a hearty confidence which made you like him before he opened his mouth.

Francine explained that we had mistakenly arrived a week early for the mythology conference. Bob said there was nothing to worry about. "We have a vacant cabin and you're more than welcome to stay. You won't feel too out of place. Physics is a kind of mythology."

Borges found that amusing. "In the ancient world the two were indistinguishable," he said. "The earliest philosophers— Pythagoras comes to mind—constructed myths to explain the cosmos. Only in the last two hundred years have science and mythology parted ways—or so they choose to believe."

Bob enjoyed a hearty laugh at that. "You'll find a lot going on here that you'll be interested in. Can we count on your staying?"

Borges was quick to accept the invitation, without consulting me, of course, though if he had I might have objected. Hanging around in the woods for several days at a conference on theoretical physics would have been the last item on my life's agenda. He stated his name and bowed slightly (he never shook hands if he could avoid it), before adding: "Poet, writer of fictions, and former Director of the National Library of Argentina."

With that cue, Bob regaled us with his own autobiography, listing all his academic honors and titles going back thirty years, while his wife rolled her eyes and smoked another cigarette. Then he pointed toward the other two men. "I'd like you to meet a couple of my colleagues: Carl Metzengerstein of Princeton University, and Victor Kravitz, of Harvard."

Carl and Vic were both a generation younger than Bob. I liked Vic right away. With his wire-rimmed glasses, his thin, unkempt beard, and his wan but friendly smile, he gave the impression of a kindly but slightly out-of-date hippie. Carl couldn't have been more different. He was a short, unattractive man with his eyes set too close together and a voice that dripped sarcasm even when he introduced himself. He was dressed all in black and his hair was brushed straight back. I couldn't help but wonder if he slept in a coffin.

We exchanged a few pleasantries with Vic. He seemed fascinated by the idea that a South American poet and his clerk—that's how Borges described me—had serendipitously appeared at the physics conference. "What is the probability of that happening?" he asked nobody in particular.

"I would say it's very strong," Borges replied. "A probability of one, in fact, since it did happen."

"Ah, then everything that happens has a probability of one?"

"Of course. That's why it happens."

Vic seemed delighted with this tautology. "Then you must be here for a reason!" he laughed.

"I'm sure I am. Only time will tell what it is."

At that time we were unaware that physicists have divided themselves into sects of believers, not unlike the scholastic philosophers of the middle ages. Vic, it seemed, was an adherent of the superdeterminism school, which believes in a kind of fate. His own fate, as it happened, was deeply entangled with that of Borges, though none of us could have suspected it then. Only later would we grasp the importance of what he said next.

"I'm having everyone over to my cabin for drinks after dinner. I hope the two of you will be able to join us."

"It would be a pleasure," Borges replied, bowing slightly.

"Great. It's Cabin No. 6. Come over around eight."

By this time I was so hungry that the mere mention of dinner sent my stomach into contractions. Fortunately Bob Morrison also invited us to the buffet dinner that would soon be served in another part of the building. Before Borges and I ventured to the dining room, we found our cabin—Bob had given me the keys to Cabin No. 9—and I hauled our luggage inside. The atmosphere was Spartan: a single room containing two single beds, a low bureau and a couple of wooden chairs, with a plank floor, knotty-pine-paneled walls, and faded calico curtains. It was cold and smelled of mice. I adjusted the thermostat on the gas-powered space heater so it would warm the place up while we were out.

Dinner was an informal buffet of fried chicken, potato salad, cole slaw and apple pie. I filled plates for Borges and myself and found seats at a round table already occupied by Vic Kravitz and three of the other physicists. Vic welcomed us to the table and introduced us to Daniel Rienzo, Eugene Takeda and Alice Demarest, all of whom had studied under Bob Morrison at MIT. As the only woman in the group, Alice naturally attracted my attention. She was in her early thirties, with straight blond hair, a delicate face and a pair of bright, probing eyes. She greeted us warmly and made a point to include us in the conversation. Sitting close beside Vic, she occasionally whispered in his ear. It seemed obvious that they were more than professional colleagues.

Borges, though blind and well into his seventies, remained a devotee of female beauty, which he fancied he could discern in a woman's voice. I sometimes wondered if what he perceived in this fashion was a reflection of quixotic folly on his part (our later encounter with Alexandra Duke confirmed that suspicion). But in the case of Alice Demarest his intuition was correct. She was a beautiful, slender woman, which made me wonder how she held her own among all these men. We later learned that she had a black belt in karate and an IQ of 168.

The other two physicists at the table, though unlike Vic and Alice, were also friendly and welcoming. Daniel Rienzo, tall, long-limbed and boyishly handsome, combined a naive, head-in-the-air charm with an aura of scientific seriousness. Even at that first meeting I detected the gleam of zealotry in his crystal blue eyes. Eugene Takeda was a Japanese-American at a time when Asians were relatively uncommon on the east coast. When he talked about physics he spoke with animation and quiet authority; the rest of the time he was reserved and exceedingly polite.

There was one part of the conversation that took on an unexpected importance in retrospect. Daniel Rienzo, perhaps not realizing that Borges was blind, peered into his clouded eyes with an ingratiating smile. "Just think," he said. "Someday you'll be able to say you had dinner with Victor Kravitz before he was famous."

"And he with me," Borges replied modestly. "Before I stopped being famous."

Daniel ignored the joke and went on. "He's working on a theory that will probably win him the Nobel Prize. It could be the 'Final Theory of Everything' that we've all been striving toward. But he keeps it a secret—from everybody but Alice, of course."

"It's not a secret," Vic said pleasantly. "It just isn't ready to go public. When I finish the calculations and publish them, it will change the landscape of physics forever."

"Even I haven't seen all the calculations," Alice told Daniel, with a slight, dismissive smile.

"They must be private indeed."

Eugene glanced across the room, where Bob and Francine Morrison enjoyed a spirited conversation with Carl and a few others we hadn't met. "Bob thinks you stole the idea from him," he said quietly.

Vic laughed. "Bob only says that because he doesn't understand it, and couldn't even imagine it. I shouldn't have told him anything about it until I was ready to publish."

"Maybe he's a little jealous," Eugene said.

"Maybe he has a lot to be jealous about," Daniel said, eyeing Alice suggestively. He quickly turned away and Alice changed the subject. Maybe Daniel was the jealous one, I thought. Not that it made any difference.

Vic was the first to finish his meal and the first to excuse himself—he needed to straighten up his cabin before people started coming over for drinks. "See you at eight? Cabin No. 6."

2.

Needless to say, Borges and I were the last to arrive at the party. In addition to Vic, the physicists we had met—Alice, Daniel, Eugene, Carl—were already there, along with Bob and Francine Morrison. Also present was a brown speckled cat, nestling comfortably on its bed beside the heater. The cabin was just like ours, except that Vic had rounded up a few more chairs and converted the top of the bureau to a bar boasting an array of wines and liquors, from which he dispensed drinks to order. The physicists drank as if they believed that time and space were relative and the next morning would never come. Whatever was in those drinks, all I can say for sure is that I drank one too many.

Our physicist friends were all experts on quantum mechanics, the theory developed by Bohr, Heisenberg, Pauli and others in the 1920s and 30s to explain the inner workings of the atom. For some reason they seemed to believe that it was essential for Borges to understand this theory, possibly to enrich his knowledge of mythology. As it happened, one of the foundational texts of quantum mechanics is a fable about a cat—the famous "Schrödinger's cat experiment"— elaborated by physicist Erwin Schrödinger in a letter to Einstein in 1935.

Eugene Takeda sat down beside Borges and explained the Schrödinger's cat experiment as follows. "According to quantum theory," he said, "particles like electrons are in superposition, which means that they exist in every possible state until you measure them, at which point they collapse into a particular state. Schrödinger didn't like this idea— neither did Einstein—and he devised his famous cat experiment in an effort to debunk it. He imagined a sealed box containing a cat and an apparatus which, if a certain quantum event occurred—specifically, the emission of a radioactive particle—a poison was released that would kill the cat."

"You see why I hate Schrödinger?" Alice said. "Killing a cat for no better reason than to prove a point!"

"Alice, it's a thought experiment," Bob said, rolling his eyes. "That means it didn't really happen."

"In some sense it happened," Daniel disagreed. "In some sense, everything that could happen *does* happen."

"Not this time!" Bob laughed. "It's a fantasy!"

"A fantasy about the needless killing of a cat is not funny," Alice insisted.

Eugene raised his hands to call time out. "Okay, kids! Do you mind if I finish? I'm just trying to explain this to Mr. Borges."

The squabbling subsided and Eugene continued. "There was a fifty percent probability that the particle would be released and thus that the imaginary cat would die," he said. "The experimenter had no way of knowing whether this actually happened until later, when he looked into the box, at which point he could determine whether the cat was dead or alive. Now here's the point of the experiment. According to quantum theory, until the experimenter was at least capable of observing the result, the cat was *both* dead and alive."

"That's palpably absurd," Borges said. "And, I might add"—tipping his head toward Alice—"inhuman."

"Schrödinger thought it was absurd as well, as did Einstein. That was his point. But he was wrong about that. The result is consistent with quantum theory, which has been proven correct in so many ways."

"There's a hidden flaw in the logic, though," Vic said, speaking up for the first time. Until then he'd hardly seemed to be paying attention.

"Come on, Vic," Bob challenged him. "You're not disputing quantum theory, I hope."

"Yes, I guess I am," Vic said. "And I'm in good company. You've heard of Von Neumann's Catastrophe, I assume?"

"Just some mathematician's daydream," Bob scoffed. "Von Neumann wasn't a physicist."

"No, but he wasn't just 'some mathematician' either."

Bob frowned at being contradicted. "Let's move on to something else," he said evenly. "Mr. Borges doesn't want to hear this shop talk."

"To the contrary," Borges said. "I've heard of Von Neumann, and I'd like to know what sort of catastrophe he lent his name to."

There was a moment of uncomfortable silence as the power relations in the room shifted to a new balance. Bob was the leader of the group and Borges had supported Vic against him, as he had supported Alice. The younger physicists seemed to be holding their breath, as if, like the cat in the box, they didn't know whether they were dead or alive.

It was Francine, Bob's wife, who broke the ice. "Go ahead, Vic," she said, lighting a fresh cigarette. "Tell us about this catastrophe of Von Neumann's."

Just then something happened that defused the tension even further. Vic's speckled cat, not to be outdone by Schrödinger's, demanded his attention by scratching and meowing at the door. He hurried over and let her out.

"Does the cat stay out all night?" Alice asked him.

"No, she doesn't like the cold. Before I go to bed, I let her in and she sleeps next to the heater." He pointed to the gas heater in the corner, identical to the one in our cabin. A cushioned cat bed was nestled against it.

"Do you have mice in here?" Eugene asked. "My cabin is teeming with them."

"Not since I found that cat. She chased them away in short order."

There was some chatter about the mice in the cabins and how lucky Vic was to have the cat. I glanced at Borges and could see him drifting away. He had no use for pets—especially cats, which he considered a species of vermin—and even less for conversations about them. I was afraid he would say something rude.

"Actually the cat found me," Vic said. "Just showed up one night and I adopted her."

"What if she doesn't come in before you go to bed?" Bob asked.

"Oh, she always comes in. The trick is not to feed her quite as much as she wants at dinner time. And then before I go to bed, I entice her back inside with a cat yummy. You know, those special treats that are made just for cats?"

"They adore them!" Alice agreed.

I knew that would be too much for Borges. "Can we get back to Von Neumann's Catastrophe?" he asked, raising his voice, and I gave a silent sigh of relief when Vic took this cue to return to the unsentimental world of math and physics.

"Sure," he said. "Von Neumann showed that there's a flaw in the basic model of quantum uncertainty, as illustrated in the Schrödinger's cat experiment. It's fundamental to the theory that nothing can be said to have happened inside that box until it was observed, or at least capable of being observed—"

"Are you saying that the physical universe has no reality apart from observation?" Borges interrupted.

"In a sense, yes."

'Esse est percipi: to be is to be perceived. The doctrine of idealism, expounded by Bishop Berkeley in the eighteenth century. Was that the view of Von Neumann?"

"Not at all. Von Neumann didn't doubt the existence of the physical universe. But he pointed out that the observer— whether a person or an instrument of some kind—is also a quantum system, whose functioning can only be determined by another observation, which is subject to the same uncertainty as the observation of the cat, and that observation in turn is subject to yet another one, and so on *ad infinitum.*"

Borges's face glowed with excitement. He had a weakness for any theoretical formulation that ended with *ad infinitum.* "An infinite regress," he muttered.

"Yes. The full name of the paradox is Von Neumann's Catastrophe of the Infinite Regress."

"Do you think it's correct?"

"I think Von Neumann had the right idea but he didn't take it far enough."

"Infinity isn't far enough?" Carl mocked.

"In my opinion Nagarjuna came closer to the truth than Von Neumann." Vic said no more. I recalled his reluctance to discuss his breakthrough work until it was ready for publication.

"I'm not familiar with Nagarjuna's work," Bob said hesitantly. "I assume he's Romanian, judging from his name—"

"He was a Buddhist sage of the first century," Borges said, "who spoke in paradoxes similar to Zeno's."

Silence again. The silence of astonishment, awkwardness, and awe. Everyone admired Vic and his research, and we were guests in his cabin. No one but Carl would have considered mocking him.

"Berkeley avoided the infinite regress by putting God at the end of the chain of observers," Borges went on. "Otherwise his idealism would have been a *mise en abîme,* as is evidently the case with your quantum mechanics."

They were all trying hard to be polite. "I'm sorry?" Eugene said.

"There's a particular kind of labyrinth that derives from pure thought," Borges said. "As a child I discovered a tin of Droste cocoa which portrayed a nurse carrying a tray on which stood an identical but much smaller Droste tin, which in turn portrayed an even smaller version of the same nurse carrying the same tin, and so forth (I assumed) to infinity. I imagined that if I stared at that tin long and deeply enough I could gaze into eternity. And since that time I have found innumerable instances of the same phenomenon, which has a name in the French language—*mise en abîme,* which means 'placed in an abyss.' And indeed, when you think deeply about such things, you fall into an abyss of infinite regression. That's what Von Neumann was talking about."

"These problems go away if you think of the universe as a single probability function," Daniel said cryptically.

"Yes, of course. That was exactly the tactic taken by Parmenides in the fifth century B.C. He held that the universe is all one thing, and therefore all movement and change are illusory. His disciple Zeno showed in his paradoxes that you quickly fall into a *mise en abîme* if you try to prove that movement and change really exist."

"Another way around it," Daniel pursued, "is the many worlds theory of Hugh Everett—"

"I beg your pardon," Borges broke in, "it was Democritus who came up with that theory, in the fourth century. And of course Giordano Bruno in the sixteenth century of our era."

"No, seriously, " Daniel said, as if he thought Borges was joking, "the many worlds theory as advanced by Everett avoids Von Neumann's infinite regress objection quite elegantly."

"And what, may I ask, is this many worlds theory, if not the same one that was proposed by Democritus and Bruno?"

"Basically, when something happens, the world splits, resulting in one world where it happens and another world where it doesn't happen."

Borges made no response to this astonishing statement. "All possibilities exist and continue to exist," Daniel went on, his tone both naive and condescending. "Schrödinger's cat didn't have nine lives—she had an infinite number of lives. That can be proven mathematically."

The sinister Carl took this as his cue to insinuate himself into the conversation. "If you really believe that, Daniel," he said, "why don't you play Russian roulette?"

As Carl spoke, to everyone's amazement, he drew a revolver from his jacket pocket, emptied one of the bullet chambers into his palm, spun the cartridge, and offered it to Daniel, who nervously waved it away.

"What's the matter?" Carl taunted. "If the gun doesn't fire, you'll survive. If it does fire, your double will survive in a different world and won't even know what happened in this one. In fact, according to the many worlds theory you could keep firing over and over again and there would always be one of you who'd survive."

Daniel seemed to have anticipated that objection. "In that event," he smiled, "I'm sure everyone here—even you, Carl—would be devastated. I wouldn't want to inflict that on you."

"I think we could take it," Carl said, "knowing you were still alive in another world."

"Carl, stop it," Bob said. "Put that gun away."

"Hugh Everett thinks he's immortal, you know," Alice observed, adding, for my benefit: "The man who came up with the many worlds theory. He works for the Pentagon now, trying to find a way to destroy the whole world without anyone noticing."

"And why not?" Carl shrugged. "Why not murder everybody if we can escape into another world?"

A few gasps, then silence. It was as if the temperature had suddenly dropped to absolute zero. Nothing moved but Carl's hand, still gesturing with the gun.

"We can all be thankful you don't believe in the many worlds theory," Bob finally said. "You probably would have blown us all away by now."

"How do you know I didn't?" Carl laughed. "For all you know, you're living in a version of the world where we all survived!"

"Put the gun away. Nobody wants to play Russian roulette tonight."

Once again it was Francine who defused the situation. "Does anybody have a cigarette?" she asked, and Eugene leaned forward to offer her one. She took her time lighting it and smoked in the most unseemly way possible, puffing like a French *courtisane,* blowing smoke rings, tipping the ashes into Bob's jacket pocket for lack of an ashtray, with no resistance from him or even a hint of disapproval. He'd been the one who stood up to Carl, but his wife, it seemed, could do no wrong.

Borges and I stayed until about ten o'clock, by which time he had successfully demonstrated, to his own satisfaction, that there was nothing in the revolutionary physics of the twentieth century which had not already been discovered by some ancient philosopher. In addition to the single wave function (Parmenides), nonobjectivity (Berkeley), and the many worlds theory (Democritus), which I've already mentioned, there was Heisenberg's uncertainty principle (obviously cribbed from Zeno's arrow paradox), entanglement (Leibniz's windowless monads), and space/time relativity (see Vedanta, Mahayana Buddhism, and the Kabbalah).

The physicists remained unimpressed. "What we're doing is science, not philosophy," Daniel said condescendingly.

"Our theories may seem wacky, but they've all been proven mathematically."

"Ah, yes, but what is mathematics? Isn't it a kind of philosophy?"

"Hardly," Daniel said dismissively, exchanging embarrassed glances with his colleagues. But he must have sensed that he stood on weak ground: as Borges went on I saw the flicker of panic in his eyes.

"The truths of mathematics must surely be a kind of philosophy," Borges said, "for they would be exactly the same if the physical world didn't exist. In view of that, how could the fundamental principles of physics be proven mathematically?"

Daniel hesitated, having grasped, too late, that arguing with Borges was a *mise en abîme* that made Von Neumann's Catastrophe look like child's play.

Borges beamed his friendliest smile. "Science, properly considered, is the battle against the bewitchment of the intelligence by mathematics." He flicked his hand toward me and stood up to leave. "I fear that the battle has been lost."

3.

We made our way back to our cabin along a gravel path that was barely visible on that moonless night. Mice scuttled out of sight as I opened the door, leaving their droppings and their smell behind. It was cold inside the cabin; I turned up the thermostat on the heater, hoping that Borges would want to go straight to bed. Instead, even after all we'd had to drink, he insisted on having his customary nightcap before retiring. I poured a couple of whiskies and we made ourselves as comfortable as we could on the two straight-backed wooden chairs.

"I might have gone a little hard on those poor physicists," Borges said after a while. "Mathematics is their version of Platonism: a world of forms that underlies material reality but is not part of it. But we're entitled to ask: where do those forms exist, if not in the material world? Is there some other world?"

"I assume they think that math is a map of reality, not reality itself," I said, downing my whisky in a single gulp.

"How can it be a map of reality, and not be part of reality? Does the reality it maps include itself?"

"I don't think I'm following this."

"That's a good thing. It's a *mise en abîme*. Follow it and it will lead you down the rabbit hole."

It might have been the rabbit hole or it might have been the alcohol I'd consumed—I felt my head (or it might have been world) rotating slowly, as if losing my balance even while sitting down. The strains of a country western song ran through my mind as I took another sip of scotch. *I was looking back to see if you were looking back to see if I was looking back to see if you were looking at me...*

"You'll find a *mise en abîme* in certain paintings by Vermeer and Velasquez," Borges went on, "in mirrors facing mirrors, dreams within dreams, maps that include maps of the territory depicted on them. And of course in the 602nd night of the *Thousand and One Nights*."

This litany filled me with a nameless dread. I thought of Von Neumann's Catastrophe, and imagined the vast universe spiraling back into the black hole that gave birth to the Big Bang. Mirrors facing mirrors, dreams within dreams, Chuang Tzu dreaming of a butterfly and wondering if he was a butterfly dreaming of Chuang Tzu. It was as if our world existed only in one of Borges's fantastic tales, or worse, a story by Poe or H. P. Lovecraft. I thought of Diotima, the waitress I'd idealized in Somerville, and of Lucinda, the lovely librarian in New York, and of course of Katie, Katie most of all. Their faces seemed to blend as I whirled down the rabbit hole.

Borges droned on, utterly oblivious to my plight. "Whenever there's something in the universe that *contains* or *depicts* the entire universe," he said, "you have a *mise en abîme*. In Jewish mysticism, for example, the first letter of the Hebrew alphabet, the *aleph,* is said to contain the entire universe; in Islam, the Quran asserts that it—the Quran—predates the Creation. And we can't overlook the Creation itself, reputedly by an omniscient and omnipotent deity who conceived in one instant not only the universe but its entire future, including the infidels and heresiarchs who would deny his existence, the false doctrines they would preach, the refutations of those doctrines, and the refutations of those refutations. Under any form of determinism, the entire universe and its future must exist in every moment of time and every corner of space."

His voice turned in circles, wheels within wheels. Time and space devouring each other like snakes. I wondered if the room would ever stop making me dizzy.

"In all such conceptions, the parts of the universe reflect and embody the whole. Thinking about them is like staring at that Droste cocoa tin. You feel yourself being whirled down into an abyss."

"Yes," I muttered, but I was so far down in the abyss that I doubt if he heard me.

"And the theories our physicist friends have put forward leave me with the same sense of vertigo. They are searching for a formula, a code, a magic key, that will unlock the secrets of the universe. But nothing within the universe can give a full account of it. Our minds would have to be as big as the universe in order to grasp it in its totality. Did you notice any such minds at the cocktail party? I did not."

Borges rattled his ice cubes like castanets in an Argentine tango, startling me out of my swoon. I tried to stand up to get more whisky but my legs would not cooperate. "The idea that the material world is an illusion," he went on, "that there must be something more primal, more permanent, more *real* behind it, is the oldest idea in religion and philosophy. What is real? Pythagoras said it was number, Thales said it was water, Anaximenes opted for air. Parmenides, coming close to the Indian Vedantists, said there is only one thing, which accordingly cannot be named or described. If you think those ideas are absurd, what do you make of modern physics?"

Undoubtedly a *mise en abîme,* I thought, if not a can of worms. I held my tongue.

"They will tell you in all seriousness that every time a particle does one thing rather than another, the world splits into two nearly identical worlds, which each continue to exist until they in turn split, and so on to infinity—a labyrinth of forking paths beyond the wildest imaginings of Democritus or Bruno, or even of myself. And those who reject that theory will argue that a cat can be both dead and alive."

That was definitely where I drew the line. If Schrödinger's cat was dead, it was because she'd used up her nine lives and she would stay dead. She would not have an infinite number of other chances. I stood firm with Alice against experimentation on animals, even imaginary ones, which in my present condition were just as real as real ones, if not more so.

"My credulity, though vast, has its limits." Borges sounded like Dr. Johnson kicking a rock to refute Bishop Berkeley. Was he having an uncharacteristic bout of common sense?

My hopes rose—a dose of common sense was just what I needed to escape from the abyss. But it was not to be. "Chesterton claimed that a man who doesn't believe in God will believe in anything," Borges said. "These physicists illustrate why it is necessary to believe in God, even if he doesn't exist."

I'm not sure if Borges really said that. If he did, I had no idea what it meant or whether it meant anything. I lurched to my feet, collected our glasses, rinsed them out, and put them back in the cupboard. It was cold in the room and I was eager to get under the covers. I helped Borges into his pajamas, then I undressed and fell heavily into bed, dreading the hangover I would face in the morning. The heater gasped and shuddered in a vain effort to keep the cabin warm. No sooner had I pulled the covers up around me than the mice started frolicking around the room. I shouted at them; they listened politely, then resumed their fun. I threw one of my shoes and then the other, and they paid no attention. Borges cursed at them in Spanish, a language which they apparently did not understand. Naturally our fancy turned to drastic remedies.

"As much as I dislike pets," Borges said, "they have their uses. I find myself coveting Vic Kravitz's cat."

"I would settle for Schrödinger's," I said. "Even a cat who's dead half the time would get rid of these mice."

Neither of us laughed. It was a lame joke which a few hours later would seem prophetic, and in incredibly poor taste.

4.

We stepped out into the fog at nine o'clock, hoping there'd be a tasty breakfast waiting for us in the main lodge, or at least a cup of hot coffee. Instead we found a police car flashing its lights in front of the entrance. A burly plainclothes cop hunched beside it, growling into a hand-held radio receiver. He eyed us suspiciously and waved us toward the door. "Everybody in the common room."

"We're not part of the physics conference," I told him.

Apparently that didn't matter. "Get the hell inside," was how he put it.

Bob Morrison hurried forward to greet us, Francine a few steps behind him. "I'm so sorry you had to be here for this," he said.

"What happened?" Borges asked.

"There's been a terrible accident," Francine said. Her eyes were bloodshot, her cheeks puffy and pale. She wore a stylish low-cut dress but she looked ten years older than she'd looked the night before.

"Vic Kravitz died in his sleep," Bob said. "He didn't come to breakfast and Alice went looking for him. Apparently there was a gas leak in his cabin."

Various emergency vehicles had arrived outside—an ambulance, a fire truck and several more police cars. Teams of investigators and safety specialists descended on Vic's cabin and fanned out around the others.

"The police want us all to stay in here while they investigate," Bob went on.

"A wise precaution in my experience," Borges said.

Bob found that amusing. "Would that be your experience as a poet? Or as a librarian?"

Borges deflected the sarcasm with one flash of his sightless eyes. "My experience as a detective."

The bewildered reaction was predictable and exactly what Borges had intended. "In addition to being a poet and librarian," I explained, "Dr. Borges is a noted detective who has investigated numerous crimes."

The physicist eyed him incredulously and smirked at his wife.

"Did you see or hear anything unusual last night?" Borges asked, jumping right into his investigation.

"I wasn't even here last night," Bob answered. "I drove back to Cambridge after dinner to pick up some slides from my office that I needed for today's program. Caught a few hours' sleep, ate breakfast at McDonald's and drove back up this morning."

Borges nodded toward Francine. "And you? Did you notice anything unusual?"

"Not really," she murmured. "It's not unusual for Bob to be sleeping somewhere else."

Bob turned his back and we followed him into the dining room. I knew that Borges, once in detective mode—and especially after his credentials as a detective had been challenged—would continue his investigation until he solved the crime, even if the police declared that no crime had been committed. With a thorough enough investigation, he once told me, some sort of crime can always be uncovered. The physicists, who undoubtedly regarded him as an amusing eccentric, had no idea what they were in for. They huddled around the table where the buffet supper had been served the night before, talking in low voices as they nibbled breakfast rolls and sipped coffee from styrofoam cups. One of their fellows had suddenly died, and they seemed to be taking it in stride, except for Alice, who sat along the wall sobbing and wiping her eyes. I guided Borges to an armchair near the table and we both sat down.

After about fifteen minutes the police officer we'd seen outside—he identified himself as Detective Blake—came through the door and raised his voice to get the crowd's attention. "Our preliminary investigation suggests that Mr. Kravitz's death was the result of accidental gas inhalation," he said. "The coroner and the forensics team are completing their work and should be able to announce the result within the hour. In the meantime we're asking everybody to stay here so you'll be available for questioning in case the need arises. We're checking the heaters in all the cabins, but as a precaution we recommend that you sleep with a window open from now on."

"And a loaded revolver under your pillow," Carl muttered, loud enough for everyone to hear him.

It was a tasteless joke and Detective Blake was not amused. "There's no evidence of foul play," he grimaced.

"We can go, then?" Bob asked.

"As I said, please remain here until the forensic team finishes its work."

"Apparently somebody thinks it was murder," Borges said after the policeman had left.

"Carl was just joking," Bob said. "But I'm glad they're investigating. It'll clear the air, put an end to the rumors."

"Are there rumors?"

"You know how these groups are. Things get a little incestuous. Everybody's got a pet theory and they don't like it when somebody puts it down."

"Did Mr. Kravitz do that?"

"No more than anybody else. I mean, sometimes he got a little sarcastic. About that many worlds stuff that Daniel's always spouting off about, for instance, or the hidden variables that Carl pulls out of the air to make his equations balance. Oops!" He shrugged sheepishly in a pantomime of self-reproach. "Did I say that? I'm the director. I'm not supposed to take sides." He glanced around to make sure that no one had overheard him.

"So if it was murder, those are the ones you'd look at? Daniel and Carl?"

"If it was—but it wasn't. So why are we even talking about it?"

He sidled off, leaving Francine leaning against the buffet table smoking a cigarette. "Physicists are so bad at lying," she said, tipping her ashes into a styrofoam cup that was still half-full of coffee. "You can't trust them at all."

"What do you think, then?" Borges asked.

"About the murder, if there was one? Three little words: *Cherchez la femme.* There's only one woman in this group, so you don't have to search very far, do you?"

"You mean Alice?"

"She was sleeping with Vic, so isn't that where you'd start?"

"You think Alice killed him?"

"Of course not," Francine sniffed. "That's something only a man would do." I followed her gaze as she peered across the room to focus on Carl. It was hard to imagine that Alice would give Carl a second glance.

"Carl?" I said incredulously.

"Alice dumped him when she took up with Vic. If anybody had a motive, he did. And then there's Daniel."

She jabbed her pointed chin toward Daniel who seemed to be bearing the brunt of Carl's sarcasm. His blue eyes gleamed like knives.

"Poor Daniel had his hopes up but only won third place. Not that I think he would have killed Vic—at least not for that reason."

"What reason, then?"

"They all make fun of him for his many worlds theory. Personally I find it charming."

She doused her cigarette in the coffee and turned around to look for another cup. While she had her back turned I grabbed Borges's arm and pulled him toward the other side of the room. Half way across we were intercepted by Alice. "What was Francine telling you?" Alice wanted to know. "It was about me and Vic, wasn't it?"

"No... not really," I stammered.

"I loved him and I don't mind anybody knowing it."

"You have my deepest condolences," Borges said. "I too have lost many of my dearest friends."

She lowered her voice. "But were they murdered?"

"Do you think that's what happened to Mr. Kravitz?"

"I sure do. You wouldn't believe what a nest of vipers this place is."

I led Borges and Alice to one side so we wouldn't be overheard. "Who do you think is responsible?" Borges asked her.

"Well, I don't want to point fingers," she said, "but there's one person here who thought Vic had jumped ahead of him on some critical research and would have done anything to keep him from publishing it."

"And who was that?"

"I won't mention any names, but if you ask around you'll find out who I'm talking about."

"Was it Carl?" I asked her.

She scowled at the mention of Carl's name. "Carl would have killed him in a heartbeat if he thought it would advance his career. But he's not who I had in mind."

"What about Daniel?"

"Daniel wouldn't hurt a fly."

She flitted away, leaving us more confused than ever. "Are you following this?" I asked Borges. His face looked tired under his halo of thin white hair. He shook his head sadly. "Only a miracle could have saved that poor man."

My bafflement deepened. "How do you know that?"

Tottering slightly, he leaned on his walking stick. I steadied him with my hand on his elbow. "Do you see Daniel Rienzo or Eugene Takeda around here anywhere? We need to talk to them."

The two physicists huddled in a far corner of the room, absorbed in an intense conversation. They stopped talking and smiled indulgently when they saw us inching toward them at approximately the speed of a tortoise. Rather than to leave us eternally stranded in space, they stepped forward to meet us, Eugene impassive and serious, gliding like a shadow,

Daniel tall and ungainly, with his boyish face and his piercing eyes.

"Will you be sleeping with a revolver under your pillow, Mr. Borges?" Daniel asked playfully.

"No," Borges said, "but I'll have Nick beside me. He can fight off the murderer while I enjoy my nightmares."

"This is no time for jokes," Eugene said.

"Just because somebody died," Daniel chided, "does that mean we have to lose our sense of humor?"

"The policeman didn't think Carl's joke about the revolver was funny," Eugene said, "and I agree."

"Do you think Mr. Kravitz was murdered?" Borges asked him.

"I doubt it," Eugene said, "but if he was, it was probably by someone in this room. Physicists can be very cold and calculating."

"Perhaps," Borges pursued, "by someone who feared that Mr. Kravitz would get credit for an important breakthrough the murderer thought was his own?"

"You mean Bob? If that was his motive he certainly made no effort to hide it. But there's something you need to understand. Physicists tend to believe that when you understand how the universe works, everything else is easy. We've solved so many intractable mysteries that if one of us committed a murder he wouldn't expect to get away with it." A sardonic smile spread across Eugene's face. "Admittedly, Bob may not be smart enough to realize that."

"I can't imagine anybody in our group wanting to kill Vic," Daniel protested. "He was such a great guy. If there's a murderer, it has to be somebody from outside."

"Unless, of course," Eugene said with a wink, pretending not to see Carl, who had crept up behind him, "it was Carl."

Sinister is the word that comes to mind when I think about Carl Metzengerstein. His black clothes, his slicked-back hair, his Peter Lorre accent, all contributed to the effect. Nevertheless, he took Eugene's gibe in good sport. "You're wondering whether I killed Vic, aren't you?" he asked with a wide, sardonic grin. "There's a simple answer to that. I couldn't have killed him, because if I did, nobody would ever know it. It's the anthropic principle."

"That's a physics joke," Daniel explained for our benefit. "What Carl means is that there's no universe in which anyone is smart enough to catch him."

"Not that there's no such universe," Carl said. "It's just that you wouldn't be in it."

Borges called a stop to this bickering. "If you didn't do it, then who did?" he asked Carl. "Please confine your answer to the universe we're in."

"In this universe," Carl said with a triumphant leer, "there are any number of people who aren't smart enough to not get caught. Several of them are in this room. You have Bob, who has no original ideas that he didn't steal from someone else, and his lovely wife, who'd stick a knife in anyone who stands in her way, and his former lover Alice—oh, did I speak out of turn?—and of course Daniel, who thinks there are as many worlds as grains of sand on all the planets in the universe—

how can a man who believes that be trusted? Did I leave anyone out?"

"What about me?" Eugene asked.

"Give me a minute and I'll think of a reason you might have done it."

Detective Blake and three uniformed officers had entered the lodge and now stood in the door to the dining room calling for our attention. I guided Borges back to his chair, where he settled serenely, blind eyes closed, the wheels of ratiocination whirling behind them, as I could tell from the occasional twitches that wrinkled his forehead. My mind was also spinning but in a confused, uncontrolled fashion, as I tried to process the jumble of theories and accusations that had been tossed our way. Everyone in the room, it seemed, had a motive to kill Vic Kravitz—and in one of the many worlds they inhabited, probably did. And everyone, without much prompting, was perfectly willing to lay the blame on somebody else. Fortunately, I told myself, Vic's death had been an accident. The police would brief us on their investigation and send us on our way.

5.

Detective Blake waited for the crowd to settle down and raised his voice again. "Could I have your attention, please! If you're standing, please find a seat. Thank you."

I pulled up a folding chair next to Borges. His eyes were closed and he seemed on the verge of falling asleep. I nudged him and he sat up with a jolt.

"We appreciate your staying while the coroner and our forensic team completed their investigation," the detective said. "If you could stay a few minutes longer I'd like to brief you on our findings. Mr. Kravitz's body was found lying in his bed, and the coroner concluded that he died in his sleep. Also found in the cabin were the bodies of his cat, in her own bed—"

"Not the cat!" Alice blurted, visibly upset.

"I beg your pardon?"

"Never mind. Go on."

"Besides the cat, a number of dead mice lay scattered around on the floor. Mr. Kravitz, and presumably the cat and the mice, died from inhalation of propane gas, which was stored in a tank behind the cabin. The gas leaked from a rubber tube connecting the tank to the room heater, through holes which had apparently been gnawed by the mice. The time of death was approximately 4:00 a.m. Based on the volume of air space in the cabin and the size of the perforations in the gas tube, the team concluded that the gas started leaking between 1:00 and 2:00 o'clock. There's no evidence of any tinkering with the heater or the gas line, other than the perforations I mentioned. Accordingly, suicide has been ruled out as the cause of death. The cabin was completely sealed—the door and all the windows were closed and locked from the inside. There's no evidence of forced entry or any other foul play. For that reason, murder has also been ruled out. The team has concluded that Mr. Kravitz's death was a tragic accident. On behalf of the Police Department, we want to express our condolences for the loss of your friend and colleague."

I can't say this announcement came as good news, since Vic was just as dead one way or the other, but I'll admit I breathed an inner sigh of relief to hear that murder had been ruled out. To my surprise, that reaction was less than unanimous.

"Schrödinger's cat was locked in a sealed box, just like that cabin," Alice said. "There's reason to believe that *it* was murdered."

"Don't be ridiculous!" Carl scoffed. "It was a thought experiment. The cat wasn't murdered."

"In principle it was."

"Come on, Alice," Bob said. "Within the structure of the experiment, there's equal reason to believe that the cat didn't die. Until they opened the box, nobody knew whether it was dead or alive."

"It might have been both," Eugene said.

"It *was* both," Daniel said.

Detective Blake had probably been warned that physicists are wacky, and he was trying to be a good sport. His bafflement was obvious but understandable—he thought they were expressing their sympathy for the cat. "What happened to the cat was also tragic," he said, a little ironically. "Not to mention the mice. But let's not forget that there was a man who died in that cabin. We're not here to talk about a cat."

"With all respect," Borges said, in a voice of authority, "I believe that we must talk about the cat."

"Like I said—"

"The question we must answer is, Why did the cat, on this particular night and no other, let the mice gnaw on the tube?"

A long silence filled the room while everyone pondered the question, or (in my case) pondered why it was important.

"OK, answer that if you can," the detective finally said, staring into Borges's clouded eyes.

"It was, if I may say so, the cat that didn't mouse."

Only I appreciated Borges's little joke—it brought a smile to my lips. The detective and everyone else remained stone-faced. "Pray tell us why that matters," the detective said, with a note of sarcasm which did not go undetected by Borges.

He replied in a tone usually reserved for idiots or very young children. "Mr. Kravitz told us last night that he adopted the cat specifically to catch mice, and on every previous occasion that's exactly what she did. She slept next to the heater in her own bed and until last night the mice kept their distance or took the risk of being eaten. But on this one occasion, between one and two o'clock in the morning, the mice gnawed the gas tube that led to the heater. How could they have done that with the cat there? The obvious answer is that the cat was already dead."

"No," the detective objected, "you've got it all backwards. The gas wasn't released until the mice gnawed through the tube. That's when the cat died."

"Then until that time the cat must have been both dead and alive. Dead, or she wouldn't have let the mice gnaw through the tube, and alive, because the gas had still not been released."

"That's absurd."

"Of course it's absurd. The whole experiment, like Schrödinger's, was aimed at demonstrating the absurdity of its premises."

"The experiment? Are you saying it was an experiment?"

"A performance, at any rate," Borges smiled. "An attempt to create an illusion which could not be penetrated by the most brilliant minds in science. And (though it's in poor taste to say so) it was conceived and carried out as a parody of the Schrödinger's cat experiment by someone with a sense of humor, or at least a sense of theater. Undoubtedly another physicist, probably someone in this room."

The reactions expressed by the physicists ranged from incredulity to scoffing and scorn. Bob Morrison probably spoke for the group—excepting Alice—when he appealed to the detective. "I think we've heard enough from Mr. Borges," he said. "He's quite the wag, but this is no laughing matter. One of our physicists is dead."

"No one is laughing, Bob," Alice said. "I want to hear what he has to say."

Borges nodded gratefully and went on: "There's a crucial fact that can't be overlooked. The cat was dead before the mice gnawed through the tube. Which means that the cat was not killed by the gas. She was killed by something else. Poison, I have no doubt."

Another long, awkward silence suggested that he had finally made his point. The order of events described by the police made no sense. Among the physicists, incredulity had given way to bewilderment. Their eyes lighted on the detective, who frowned pensively. "How do you suppose that came about?" he asked Borges.

"I can tell you exactly how it came about," Borges said. "Last night, at a cocktail party attended by myself and several other people in this room, the nightly ritual of Mr. Kravitz and his cat was discussed. At the time I found the discussion boring and inane, but possibly for that reason I remember it quite distinctly. At about nine o'clock the cat was scratching at the door and Mr. Kravitz let her out. Someone asked him, 'Does the cat stay out all night?' 'No,' he answered, 'she doesn't like the cold. She comes in and sleeps next to the heater. That's why I don't have any mice in here. The place used to be crawling with them.'

"'What if she doesn't come in?' someone asked—I think it was the same person who had asked whether the cat stayed out all night. 'Oh, she always comes in,' Mr. Kravitz said. 'The trick is not to feed her quite as much as she wants at dinner time. And then before I go to bed, I call her back inside with one of these cat treats.' At this point, I assume, Mr. Kravitz displayed some sort of cat candy or the like."

Several people who had been present nodded their agreement. "He showed us a box of cat yummies," Alice said. "That's what he gave the cat when she came in."

Borges nodded. "And that is undoubtedly how the murderer delivered the poison to the cat, knowing her taste for such treats—and knowing how long the poison would take to kill her. Just long enough, I'm sure, to give her time to curl up in her bed beside the heater and go to sleep, dying not long afterwards. Meanwhile Mr. Kravitz had gone to sleep in his bed. Unhindered by the cat, the mice came out and nibbled through the gas line, releasing the gas."

"This is just speculation," Daniel said. "It certainly isn't science."

"No," Borges agreed, "it's what you scientists call a hypothesis. There is a simple way to confirm or refute it—the police can perform an autopsy on the cat. If she died from gas inhalation, then I will freely admit my error. But if, as I suspect, they find some other poison in the cat's system, my hypothesis will be confirmed."

"Fair enough," Daniel said, and several others nodded in agreement.

"There's one other potential piece of evidence I'd like to consider," Borges said. "Detective Blake, in examining the rubber gas tube did you notice anything peculiar, other than the fact that it had been gnawed through?"

"Well, yes, in fact," the detective said, "though I gave it no weight at the time. There was a greasy film around the area that had been gnawed on."

"As I suspected. The murderer could not be sure that the mice would gnaw on the tube, so he or she smeared it with something to attract them. Peanut butter, or the like. That chemical analysis can also be performed in the police lab. I would also examine the cat treats box for traces of the same poison."

The detective made a face, pulled out a pocket notebook, and jotted a few notes. Obviously he was still wasn't convinced but he was willing to play along.

"So," Borges went on, "assuming these two chemical analyses show what I expect them to show, our task is to identify the murderer."

"Wait a minute," Carl blurted. "Aren't you jumping the gun? We don't know if there's even been a murder."

"As I said, assuming that the lab results show that there was."

"Well, I think we ought to wait."

"I agree," Daniel said.

Borges raised his hands in mock surrender. "As you wish. With one of your colleagues dead, I should think you'd be more interested in finding out who killed him. It's almost as if you're afraid of the answer."

"We don't know whether anybody did anything," Carl said through clenched teeth.

"I'm interested," Alice chirped. "Let's hear what he has to say."

"Yeah," Francine added. "I want to hear this."

No one wanted to overrule the two women. "Thank you," Borges said, nodding gallantly in their direction (of course he couldn't see them, but smiled as if he could). "Now, would everyone who was present at the cocktail party please raise your hand and give your name to Detective Blake."

"Now you're asking us to turn ourselves in!" Daniel said. "That's the limit. I'm not going along with this."

"Neither am I," Bob said.

"Nor I," said Carl.

"Me neither," Eugene said.

Borges waited until they had finished. "Obviously you've chosen to identify yourselves in a different way," he smiled. "Detective Blake, please note the four gentlemen who just spoke. Add to them the two ladies who spoke a few minutes ago, and we have our six suspects."

That trick nearly ignited a full-scale rebellion. All of them—now identified as suspects—were on their feet, calling out, cursing at Borges, grabbing their papers and coats. If Borges hadn't raised his walking stick I think they might have attacked him. Not having a walking stick, for a moment I feared that I might be sacrificed to their wrath. But before that could happen, order was restored by Detective Blake, who dispatched two of the uniformed officers to block the door.

"Okay, everybody," he barked. "Shut up and sit down!"

With various degrees of recalcitrance and delay—some verging on defiance—they all complied. "Okay," the detective told them, "now one at a time, raise your hand and state your name."

No one moved a muscle.

"Either that or I'm taking you all in."

Alice broke first, followed by Daniel.

"Alice Demarest."

"Daniel Rienzo."

The officer recorded the names in his notebook. Then Bob raised his hand. "OK," he laughed. "I'm the director of the program, so I guess I'd better show some leadership. Bob Morrison."

"Carl Metzengerstein." Mumbling, almost inaudible. Hatred in his eyes.

"What was that?"

"Carl Metzengerstein."

"Eugene Takeda."

Francine didn't raise her hand. "I can't believe I'm being included in this. Bob, you're the director. Can't you tell this charlatan to shut the hell up?"

"Your name please, ma'am," the detective said.

"Francine Morrison. Bob is my husband, in case you were wondering. I'm not a physicist. Doesn't that let me off?"

Detective Blake ignored the question and recorded her name in his notebook. "Let's take a five-minute break," he told the crowd. "You can get up and walk around, but nobody leaves the building. Is that clear?"

As I think back on that afternoon, I can only marvel—as I think Detective Blake must have marveled—at how masterfully Borges had taken command of the situation. Five of the most brilliant physicists in America—plus Francine Morris, who though not a physicist had shown herself to be wily and calculating—had stumbled into the range of his extraordinary vision, which was a faculty not of the eyes but of the mind. Of course only one of them was the murderer, though others may have been protecting the culprit. But whatever their level of guilt or innocence, by the time they returned to their seats they all must have known that the game Borges had set in motion would be played to its inexorable finish. There was no place to hide from his blind but all-seeing gaze.

Detective Blake called for their attention and once again Borges had the floor. "To identify the murderer is a straightforward process of elimination," he told the suspects. "In my conversations with each of you, I raised the question of who had a motive to kill Mr. Kravitz, and what that motive might have been. Most of you were eager to speculate on the others' possible motives. Only one of you—Eugene Takeda—came away from this inquiry unscathed. Nobody could think of a single reason why Eugene would have killed Mr. Kravitz."

Everyone turned to look at Eugene, who squirmed as if he'd been named as the murderer. Somehow being thought innocent was as embarrassing as being accused of the crime. "Well," he stammered. "Thanks... I guess."

"Why is that so important?" Daniel wanted to know.

"Contrary to popular fiction," Borges said, "the murderer is not usually the last person anyone would suspect of the crime. In fact—and I think you would agree, Detective Blake—it would be exceedingly rare for a murderer to be unsuspected by anyone he knows. For that reason"—he paused, as if for no better reason than to hold them in suspense—"I suggest provisionally, pending the possible discovery of contrary evidence, that we eliminate Eugene Takeda as a suspect."

Eugene sighed audibly and wiped his brow in a pantomime of relief. "Whew! Dodged that bullet!"

Some of the others laughed, others shook their heads as if they had second thoughts about excusing him. "The remaining five suspects," Borges continued, "all had a motive attributed to them by at least one other person. It's interesting to consider how many people each suspect attempted to implicate. I remember this precisely. Alice and Bob each attributed a motive to two people, Francine to three. Carl attributed a motive to all four of the others, and Daniel did not attribute a motive to anyone."

Daniel seemed as embarrassed as Eugene had been. You might have thought the others would blame Carl for accusing them, but instead they glared suspiciously at Daniel as if his failure to accuse anyone was evidence of guile or a guilty conscience. "Why does it have to be one of us?" Daniel pleaded. "That's just a baseless assumption."

"All investigations begin with assumptions," Borges said. "They are in effect part of the hypothesis, to be tested and discarded if appropriate. Let's trace this one out. Put yourself in the shoes of the murderer. Although you have taken every precaution to disguise the crime as an accident, you know that there will be an investigation, in which case you would want there to be other suspects. If given the opportunity, you would cast suspicion on others. For this reason, we can eliminate Daniel Rienzo as a suspect. He didn't name any names. I conclude—again, provisionally—that he is innocent of the murder."

As Borges's list shortened, the remaining suspects grew noticeably uneasy, even hostile. They had the feeling—quite justifiably—that they were being singled out. "We are left with the following suspects," he said equably, ignoring or more likely oblivious to their hostility.

"Alice, who implicated Bob and Carl.

"Bob, who implicated Carl and Daniel.

"Francine, who implicated Alice, Daniel and Carl.

"And Carl, who implicated everyone.

"The first of these suspects, Alice, can be eliminated immediately. Not because she was Mr. Kravitz's lover (which was the motive suggested by Francine). Lovers have been known to be quite murderous to each other on occasion. But remember that the crime was carried out through the poisoning of a cat—an actual cat, not a theoretical cat, as in Schrödinger's experiment, to which Alice, at the cocktail party, objected strenuously and I think quite sincerely. I submit that she would have been incapable of devising and carrying out a murder involving the sacrifice of a cat."

Alice nodded vigorously and the remaining three suspects struggled to keep their composure. All eyes were on them and they must have known—one of them, anyway—that their behavior during the next few minutes could mean the difference between freedom and life imprisonment. "That leaves Francine, Carl and Bob," Borges went on. "Francine implicated Alice for being Victor's lover, and Carl, who apparently has a romantic history with Alice, on grounds of jealousy. We'll come back to whether a rivalry for Alice's affections is a sufficient motive. Carl seems an obvious suspect, since he was keen to point the finger at all the others. But this reflects Carl's unsavory character more than his actions. He is an arrogant, judgmental, suspicious man who is eager to cast blame for anything that goes wrong. This does not prove his innocence, but it detracts from the probative value of his suspicions. And I would add that the motives attributed to him are themselves somewhat suspect, as we shall see.

"Now we're down to Bob and Francine, either of whom may have acted independently or with the other's knowledge or connivance. Bob is the director of this program and a physicist in his own right. He fits the profile of the murderer, who had a knowledge of physics, a sense of humor, and a flair for theater, having devised a means of killing Mr. Kravitz within the framework of the classic Schrödinger's cat experiment which the two of them had argued about."

Bob tried to laugh but it came out as a desperate cackle. "How do you think I pulled it off? Spooky action at a distance? I was a hundred and fifty miles away in Cambridge all night and I can prove it."

Borges smiled indulgently. "That apparent impossibility was part of your design. But it only worked so long as no one suspected the cat was dead. Your movements—the drive to Cambridge, the visit to your office, the breakfast at McDonald's, which you were so keen to tell us about—would have provided a perfect alibi if the murder had occurred in the middle of the night. But now we know that your physical location at the time of Mr. Kravitz's death is irrelevant. You were in the cabin when Nick and I left, and even if you left with the others you may have returned on some pretext; only your victim would have known that. Through the mechanism of using the cat—or rather the dead cat—as a triggering device, you were entangled with the cat, and through the cat, with Mr. Kravitz at the time of his death. It's quite clear that you killed him. Unless of course you want to implicate your wife."

"Don't even think about it!" Francine growled, curling her hand into a claw.

Bob's eyes bulged desperately, like particles of light trying to escape from a black hole. "You're just making this up!" he shouted at Borges. "You don't have any proof!"

A broad grin spread across Borges's face. As a matter of form, he always waited for the culprit to deny that he had any proof before he delivered his *coup de grâce*. "As you physicists have taught us," he told Bob, "there are no certainties in this world, only probabilities. It's possible that some stranger broke into Mr. Kravitz's cabin, poisoned his cat and smeared peanut butter on the gas line. It's possible that the cat committed suicide to protest being used as the subject of a sadistic thought experiment. It's possible that the world split and the true murderer escaped into another universe. But the range of reasonable doubt narrows with each additional bit of evidence that we consider. For example, you had a motive—two motives, in fact—as everyone knows. Alice named both you and Carl as the men who were jealous of Mr. Kravitz's success in winning her affections, after your own attempts had failed."

"Oh, is that right?" Francine snarled, glaring at her husband.

"And you knew that Mr. Kravitz had made an important breakthrough in the research to which you claim priority."

"It wasn't a breakthrough," Bob protested, a little too vehemently. "It was a crazy diversion into Buddhism. You heard him."

"He said you thought you should get the credit for that work," Daniel said.

"I heard that too," Eugene added.

"I didn't want credit for that nonsense!"

"You killed him before he could publish his paper," Alice said bitterly.

"I didn't want him to publish it because it would have set physics back fifty years. It would have been a humiliation for me and my department. But that doesn't mean I killed him."

"We all know you did it, Bob," Carl murmured.

Bob lurched upright, gasping for breath, gathered his papers and made ready to leave. "I don't have to listen to this."

"Other facts will come to light," Borges droned on blandly. "The poison will be detected in the cat, and the police will discover where it was obtained. Residues will be found on your clothing and in your home. Perhaps one of the neighbors noticed you visiting Mr. Kravitz's cabin before you drove to Cambridge. Nature, as you have learned, does not yield up her secrets without a struggle. But the truth about a murder cannot long remain hidden after the police begin their investigation."

Bob hurried toward the door but, unlike an elementary particle, his speed and location were easily determined by the two uniformed officers. They blocked his way and had handcuffs on him before you could say Heisenberg's Uncertainty Principle.

6.

We drove back to Boston the next morning, having shivered all night in our cabin after Borges forbade me to turn on the heater. The prospect of spending another ten days and nights in that boreal wasteland was enough to put the Nordic mythology conference far out of our minds. Not to say that our escape from the north woods was an easy one. Clouds midnight black, rain lashing down in frenzied waves, wipers scraping the windshield like the claws of wild beasts. Huge, dark evergreens dwarfing the road seemed to be lighting our way down to the land of the trolls. Borges clutched his walking stick and muttered imprecations in some language last heard in the early middle ages. At last we reached a paved road and then finally the interstate highway. I was exhausted from my labors at the helm but Borges, now relaxed, was his old chipper self, oblivious to the turbulence of the external world.

Before we left the conference center we had received an update from Alice Demarest. Bob Morrison had confessed to everything, insisting that his motive for killing Vic had nothing to do with jealousy, either sexual or professional, and that he did it for altruistic reasons, to save physics and the world from his dangerous theories. Alice had searched all night through Vic's papers and notebooks in hopes of finding a record of his breakthrough research, but she found very little. As it turned out, his final theory of everything—which might have changed the world—had died with him, except for a few indecipherable fragments.

"It's a pity Mr. Kravitz didn't live long enough to publish his work," Borges said. "Though based on what he said, it's easy to imagine what he would have written."

I gasped with incredulity. Did Borges think he could *imagine* a physical theory as if it were like writing a poem? His hubris had finally reached its limit.

Sensing my reaction, he offered a weak defense. "Physics is a kind of detective work, is it not?"

"The fundamental mysteries of nature aren't the kind a detective tries to solve," I said.

He nodded as if he agreed. But then he said, "There are no mysteries in nature. The only mysteries are in our minds. In that respect, the physicist and the detective stand on an equal footing."

That absurdity hardly merited an answer, so I held my peace. The rain was coming down hard again and I had to keep my mind on the road.

"Without a detective there is no mystery," he explained. "Was nature a mystery before man walked the earth? No, it simply *was*."

A huge truck roared past like a comet, trailing a cloud of mist and spray that almost blew us off the road. I gripped the wheel as if my life depended on it—which it did—and wondered if Borges or our physicist friends had ever encountered raw, primal nature as it really is, not in a laboratory or a poem or a thought experiment but in its own element. Could anyone who had done that think these gigantic forces existed only as possibilities?

"The detective is to a mystery what the observer was to Schrödinger's cat," Borges said. "Unless he's looking—and asking—there isn't any mystery."

"I still don't buy that when it comes to Schrödinger's cat," I said. "Let's face it, the cat was either dead or alive, regardless of whether anybody was looking at it."

"Either/or," he chuckled. "It's hard for us to think any other way. But the universe doesn't necessarily think the same way we do."

"It doesn't think at all, does it?"

"Pythagoras held that the universe exists primarily as *number*," he said after a moment. "What could that mean? A number standing alone is meaningless. It takes on meaning only as part of a series or a ratio or an equation: a relationship of some kind. The sum of all conceivable number relationships is what we call mathematics. And likewise Nagarjuna said nothing exists in itself, but only as part of a web of mutually-dependent possibilities. That's where I think Mr. Kravitz was going with his final theory of everything— back to the sources of science in ancient philosophy and religion. No doubt his theory would have revolutionized physics, if it didn't destroy it, as Bob Morrison feared. Sooner or later it probably would have driven him mad, along with everyone else who took it seriously."

"Would that include you?"

"A man who reaches my age—even an ignorant fool like me—must learn to stop asking questions that can't be answered. I'm afraid Mr. Kravitz's final theory of everything would have been another infinite regress, another *mise en abîme*. That's what every such theory will be until man can stand outside of time and space."

I went out on a limb. "That will never happen."

"No," he laughed, "which is why Bishop Berkeley located the world's existence in the mind of God. That solves the problem quite neatly. God is the final theory of everything."

It amazed me that Borges, after all his peregrinations through the paradoxes of science, mathematics and philosophy, had arrived at God as the ultimate resting point of human thought. Had I heard him correctly?

I glanced to my right, insanely taking my eyes off the road just long enough to see him enjoying a smug, self-satisfied smile. He looked like Schrödinger's cat after it ate the canary. "Of course," he said, "a cynic might be justified in asking: Is there a god beyond God, and another god beyond that one, and so on *ad infinitum?* Isn't this just another *mise en abîme?*"

∞

We had supper that night in the Oak Bar at the Copley Plaza Hotel, where the tall windows shielded us from the fury of the still-driving rain. Borges regretted missing the Nordic mythology conference but he was excited to have notched another victory in his work as a detective. He questioned me closely about how I intended to write up the case (a task I've procrastinated until now) and questioned me closely about how I intended to characterize the murderer, Bob Morrison, his wife Francine, and the victim, Victor Kravitz. Bob Morrison, though not inherently evil, was an egoist who viewed the world through the lens of his own passions. He imagined that understanding how the universe worked qualified him to judge everything that went on in it. Francine was much wiser than her husband, because she knew he was a fool. I think she suspected all along that he was the killer. As for Vic Kravitz, he had his flaws like everyone else; nevertheless he was a brilliant scientist who gave his life for the advancement of knowledge. I saw him as a tragic hero unforeseeably struck down by a caprice of fate.

"Superficially you are correct," Borges replied with highhanded insouciance. "Though his fate was hardly capricious or unforeseeable. He was brought down by the sin of hubris—overweening pride—the same fate met by Oedipus, Faust, and so many others."

I had to disagree. "He seemed very modest, I thought. Not arrogant or proud."

"Call it a kind of madness, then," Borges said. "The madness of knowledge. He sought a kind of knowledge—a final theory of everything—that is forbidden to man. But he was not a tragic hero."

The waiter arrived with our meals: crab cakes for me, braised short ribs for Borges. We savored our food, enjoyed our wine, basked in the cheerful ambience. I think we both felt lucky to have escaped from the physicists and their mad theories and obsessions. Borges sat quietly while he ate, and then, as soon as he laid down his fork, he picked up the conversation where it had left off. "In the middle ages," he said, "philosophers asked, Can God, in his omnipotence, be irrational, capricious, evil? Of course we don't ask those questions about God anymore—we ask them about the universe."

"And the answer appears to be yes," I said, thinking of Schrödinger's cat, simultaneously dead and alive.

"It has always been so. The universe, like God, can do anything it chooses. But if you probe too far into its secrets—whether out of curiosity, ambition, or Faustian pride—you will be punished."

"Then wasn't Vic Kravitz a tragic hero, like Faust and Oedipus before him?"

"Unfortunately the physicists, with their love of infinity, have made tragedy impossible. Tragedy recapitulates fate—it is not just a series of events but a *meaningful* series of events, and the meaning comes from the denouement. But in an infinite universe, no denouement is possible: your hero remains forever stuck in the middle of the story like Schrödinger's cat."

∞

Timothy is much more advanced in the work of oblivion than any of the other patients, which gives him a kind of elite status, as befits an explorer into uncharted territory. Words are abandoning him at an astonishing rate. And what is being left behind? Ideas, perceptions, sensations? Those seem to be evaporating as well. Yet his eyes tell a different story, a story that is coherent and intense, like the eyes of a sage, unfettered by language and memory, who sees deeply into the nature of things.

Our memory caretakers seem to suppose that memory defines our existence. I heard one of them say of Timothy that "his self is draining away," the implication being that once his memory is gone there will be nothing left of him. At one time—back when my memories were accumulating instead of disappearing—I shared that assumption.

Borges called himself an impostor because he believed in the nothingness of personality. In his view everyone is an impostor because the self is an illusion. "What am I?" he asked me as I drove him to Logan Airport the day after our return from New Hampshire. As usual the route was one long traffic jam, providing plenty of time for philosophical speculation. "I'm not the world of appearances," Borges said, "nor my sensory experiences; I'm not my tasting, or smelling, or desire, or happiness, or sadness, because those conditions expire without annulling me with them. And yet I am nothing without them."

"What about your memories?" I asked, thinking back on our adventure in the Amnesia Ward. "Aren't your memories what give you a continuous identity?"

"A memory is like an echo, duplicating an event that precedes it," he said. "It's not the thing we remember, but a representation, an image of the thing remembered. How can the self depend for its existence on a congeries of fading reflections?"

The mouth of the Sumner Tunnel yawned before us like the entrance to a labyrinth. Following the string of traffic we threaded our way inside, confident that fate, or determinism, or design, or perhaps blind chance would lead us to our destination.

"But those reflections," I said, "are what make you the same person from one minute to the next."

"Is that all the self is? A hall of mirrors?"

In the shadowy underworld beneath Boston Harbor we came to a halt, boxed in on all sides by huge trucks that loomed over us like prison walls. We stopped talking until the traffic began to move again and we came back up into the light.

"Pythagoras," Borges resumed, "who preached the transmigration of souls, said the reincarnated soul is the same soul even though it lacks all memory of its previous existence. The souls that Dante envisioned in paradise were blissfully oblivious of their lives on earth."

"But we don't believe in an immaterial soul anymore, do we?"

"We exist in a material world governed by physical laws. But every day we have the experience of making things happen only because we will them to happen. That's why Schopenhauer identified the *will*—the consciousness of an autonomous self—as the essence of personal identity."

I'd never liked that idea and I doubted if Borges did. It sounded Nietzschean or worse, the fantasy of a megalomaniac. Isn't enlightenment the extinction of desire, not the exaltation of it? But then what defines your personal identity, if not your will or your memory?

"There's an experience more primary than willing or remembering," Borges said, as if reading my mind, "and that is knowing."

"Knowing?"

"Knowing that you exist—that something exists—if nothing else."

"That could be an illusion. Even your memories—"

"How could consciousness of your own existence be an illusion?" he asked in a patronizing tone, as if I'd never heard of Descartes. I glanced at him just long enough to see a mischievous smile cross his face. "Unless, of course, you *are* the illusion."

∞

Katie lay in a coma for twenty-one days, her beautiful body smashed, her face battered beyond recognition. I sat beside her in my back brace, whispering, begging her to come back. Ingrid and Gracie drifted in and out. I sat beside her day after day.

After two weeks she opened her eyes and looked at me. I squeezed her hand but it was limp and insensible. "Katie," I said. "It's me."

She frowned. "Do I know you?"

Then she closed her eyes and never opened them again.

A week later the doctor called us together for a family conference. "Your mother is gone," he told Ingrid, who seemed to be in charge.

"She's still there," I said. "I saw her."

"She's paralyzed and unconscious," the doctor said. "Her brain is dead."

"She spoke to me." I couldn't bring myself to repeat what she had said.

"Did she recognize you?" the doctor asked.

I lowered my eyes.

"She's gone," Ingrid said. She nodded at Gracie and they agreed to follow the doctor's advice.

Was she really gone? Her memories were gone; she could no longer exercise her will, if it still existed. She was paralyzed and unconscious, the doctor said. Yet to me she was still there. What was left of her? I'll be finding out soon enough.

It's my fate—if I know Ingrid—to end the same way, with the flick of a switch (they don't actually unplug anything). "Don't think you can get off the hook by forgetting your sins," she told me. "Forgetting them only proves that you committed them."

Fate doesn't proceed in a straight line. It forges a labyrinthine path with many turns and twists, which nevertheless arrives infallibly at its destination. Such twists may appear ironic to those who imagine themselves standing outside of it. In fate, past, present and future exist all at once. In its inexorability lie the seeds of tragedy, as will appear in my third story—the last one I will ever write about Borges, since it concerns his last case. It is entitled, "An Ironic Twist of Fate."

An Ironic Twist of Fate

And shake the yoke of inauspicious stars
From this world-weary flesh...

—Shakespeare, *Romeo and Juliet*

Late in the summer of 1975, a letter arrived from Buenos Aires containing detailed instructions which seemed more like a command than a request. Borges was coming to Boston to participate in a conference on Cervantes at the Boston Public Library. The conference organizers would pick him up at the airport and bring him to the Copley Plaza Hotel. I was to meet him there and escort him to the conference. I should expect to spend the weekend with him and then put him on a plane to Norman, Oklahoma, where another conference would welcome him.

I took the day off from work and drove downtown. It seemed an ordinary morning, a foggy Friday in September, threatening rain. Puffs of mist curled through the streets, muffling the traffic noise. The tops of the tallest buildings were lost in the clouds. There was no reason to suspect that anything calamitous was about to happen. But as is so often the case, the surface of things belied the underlying reality.

Fate or its embodiment in human agency had set its course on a crime that would prove as dangerous to Borges as to its intended victim. His prowess as a detective, his Platonic ideals and his code as a gentleman—all would be sorely tested, with tragic results. It was the last time we would spend together.

I found him in his hotel room, waiting for lunch to be brought up by room service. He wore a dark blue double-breasted suit that would have been stylish in the 1940s, which is probably when he bought it. We exchanged greetings and caught up on our small talk, and he briefed me on the conference. As usual, he intended to keep his participation to a minimum, delivering a brief talk on Cervantes's treatment of the circularity of time in *Don Quixote*. I had no idea why he wanted me to be there, other than to serve as his seeing-eye dog. Surely at such a low-key event there would be no murders or other crimes that I would be expected to write up.

The television was on, with the volume set low. He asked me to turn it up, and when I did he aimed his blind stare at it as if carefully scrutinizing the picture. A local news show was in progress. The newscaster—a ravishing blonde with puffy hair and a doe-eyed smile—was describing a devastating pile-up on the Massachusetts Turnpike, which had been caused, she said, by an "ironic twist of fate."

Borges scoffed, as he often did while pretending to watch television. "News reporters seem to believe in fate," he said, "but it's only newsworthy when it twists. It can march blithely forward day after day, pulling the levers of power like a vast secret society— toppling governments, manipulating stock markets, enriching some, impoverishing others—but it's only news when it twists, and even more so when it twists ironically."

"Man bites dog," I said. "Happens all the time."

"But you realize, of course, that if fate exists, then every dog who ever bit a man was obeying its commands, just as surely as the exceptional man who bit a dog?"

"Of course."

"No irony is necessary for fate to do its work. It operates in plain view, without raising an eyebrow."

"It sounds like you believe in fate."

"A blind man may be forgiven for feeling a kinship with fate, which is also said to be blind. We are brothers, he and I, though not always friends. I sympathize with his false starts and hesitations, his awkward attempts to conceal his blindness behind a veil of purpose and foresight. Does he stumble, plod doggedly forward, make a wrong turn—and then, realizing his mistake, do an about-face and march the other way? Does he step on peoples' toes, brush them aside, send them away cursing under their breath?"

"No doubt," I said, thinking more of Borges than of fate.

"And then there's blind chance, which is perhaps the opposite of blind fate. Like all opposites they co-exist. Imagine two blind men wandering in a labyrinth, tapping out their separate paths, hoping not to collide in some paradoxical meeting place." He wandered momentarily in his own mental labyrinth. "Fury is also said to be blind..."

"As are alleys, investment pools, and obedience," I pointed out.

"And love," he smiled. "It can override your will and determine the course of your life, so it is in fact a kind of fate."

I was surprised to hear him speak of love, which wasn't one of his usual interests. He must have sensed my surprise. "You forget that I am a Latin American man," he said. "From time immemorial, a beloved woman has been part of every Latin man's fate. I need only cite Don Quixote's Dulcinea."

"Who didn't exist."

"No matter. His love for her, and the tribulations he suffered on her account, were real enough."

"Don Quixote didn't exist either."

"Yet he is immortal," Borges smiled. "If you'll pardon a poet's testament of faith."

He dug his walking stick into the carpet, pushed himself upright, and stalked to the window, as if to demonstrate that he could make his way unassisted through the real world. "Of course in expressing my kinship with fate," he said after a moment, "I speak as a poet. As a detective I take an altogether different view. A detective cannot believe in fate. He must believe in free will and human agency. A detective who believes in fate would be a mere soothsayer, like Tiresias. Instead of searching for clues, he would examine the entrails of chickens."

Before I could think of a witty reply, a room service waiter knocked and pushed his cart into the room. I turned off the TV and settled down to watch Borges eat his lunch (a chicken salad sandwich, without the entrails). None being offered to me, I contented myself with a glass of water. The conversation moved off in a different direction, to my regret: we had barely scratched the surface of his dual nature— detective and poet, intrepid rationalist and blind Latin lover of nonexistent women. But we would have ample opportunity to revisit those topics later. In an ironic twist (I won't say of what), he would soon fall to the bewitchment of fate and a love not unlike Don Quixote's for the fair Dulcinea.

The Boston Public Library is about three blocks from the Copley Plaza, a good hour's walk at Borges's tortoise-like pace. As we walked he revealed the real reason he'd invited me to attend the conference. "It is my fate," he said, "to spend the coming weekend with the French postmodern novelist and critic Philippe Moreau, at the country house of Maximilian Duke, the newspaper mogul, and his wife, Alexandra."

"Your fate?" There was that word again.

"'Curse' might be a better word. Alexandra Duke wrote me a very flattering invitation several months ago and I foolishly accepted it, not imagining that Moreau would be there. It seems the two of them are friends."

"You don't like Moreau?"

"He is my bitterest enemy, resulting from a review I published in 1954 of his book on Herbert Quain. Putting him and me in the same country house for the weekend is indeed an ironic twist of fate, if not the prelude to the kind of murder which, according to Agatha Christie, usually takes place on such occasions. Will you accompany me?"

"You want me to spend the weekend with you at the Dukes' country house?"

"Yes, of course."

"Will I be there as a witness or a victim?"

"If all goes well, you'll be there as the assistant to the detective who solves the murder."

"Whose murder?"

"It would be impolitic of me to speculate."

Impolitic or not, he pivoted back to Moreau without missing a beat. "You'll meet Moreau this afternoon at the conference. He is a first-class charlatan who will stop at nothing to advance his career. He claims to have been born in Avignon, but his actual birthplace was Montpellier. His mother was a Tyrolese washerwoman, not a Polish aristocrat, and when the Resistance tried to recruit him he feigned deafness. His autobiography is a tissue of lies. Even his novels are fictitious."

Borges rapped his walking stick on the sidewalk to underscore his outrage at that last transgression. "And if that were not enough, he fancies himself a detective and touts himself as my superior in that department."

At the Library we spent another thirty minutes climbing the stairs, locating the auditorium, and installing Borges in his seat behind the long table on the podium. The topic was Cervantes and Don Quixote; the panelists consisted mostly of deluded academics all too eager to follow in the footsteps of the Castilian madman. As usual I wondered why I had accompanied Borges on this journey.

Philippe Moreau was one of the panelists. He was about twenty years younger than Borges—in his mid-fifties, I guessed—with faded blue eyes and shoulder-length gray hair that looked slightly comical on a man his age. He wore an expensive tweed jacket over a navy turtleneck and wire-rimmed glasses of the type popularized by John Lennon. Like all French theorists, he talked a lot about "texts" and mentioned Marx or Freud in every sentence. His presentation centered on a Cervantes-impersonator called Avellaneda who, nine years after the publication of *Don Quixote,* published a spurious "second volume" purporting to continue the story of the ingenious knight. A year later Cervantes published his own Part II, in which he attacked Avellaneda's work (keeping up the pretense that Part I was factual) as a tissue of lies. Even Don Quixote, the character, was offended by the spurious book. In Chapter 59, he encounters two gentlemen who claim to have read it, and he is outraged to learn that it depicts him as having renounced his love for Dulcinea.

Such narrative convolutions seemed made to order for a French theoretician. "The interweaving of these two texts— clearly a signifier for unresolved Oedipal conflict—might be called the original metafiction," Moreau intoned. "A character in a novel—the madman Don Quixote—meets two equally fictitious readers of a different novel purporting to be about himself and denies that it represents the truth. As readers, how can we know which of these fictional madmen to believe? Does 'truth' have any meaning in this pre-capitalist world before literary creation became commoditized?"

Somewhere in the middle of this gobbledygook my eyes glazed over, but I heard enough to understand where it led. Just as Don Quixote was outraged by Avellaneda's disparaging his love for Dulcinea, Cervantes himself was outraged by the impostor's inferior and imitative book—so much so that he had Don Quixote die at the end of Part II to ensure that no more sequels could be written.

"But just who was this Avellaneda?" Moreau asked rhetorically. "Scholars have spent over four hundred years asking that question, but to me the answer is obvious: Avellaneda was Cervantes himself. First he publishes a book about a fictional madman called Don Quixote; then, pretending to be a writer named Avellaneda, he publishes a sequel in which Don Quixote ends his life in a lunatic asylum. He denounces the sequel as despicable and false, and publishes Part II, a second sequel, in which Don Quixote denounces the first sequel for disparaging his love for a woman who did not exist, even as a fictional character, in either book. The scheme can only be described as Borgesian."

All eyes were on Borges, who maintained a marmoreal calm, as if to acknowledge Moreau's existence would have been conceding too much.

During the break, I escorted Borges to the refreshments table and poured him a seltzer water, fending off well-wishers who wanted to shake his hand. Moreau cut his way through the crowd and tugged at Borges's sleeve. "I hope you weren't embarrassed by my little *hommage,*" he said. "After all, how many writers have an adjective named after them? Kafka, Dickens, Orwell...."

"Moreau," Borges smiled. "Isn't that where 'moronic' came from?"

"Ah, such a joker! You're so much like Cervantes. You've even got an Avellaneda of your own. Did you know that?"

"What are you talking about?"

"Then you haven't seen the sequel to your detective stories? I thought you might have written it yourself, or"—he shot a glance at me—"did you have your Watson do it?" He started to walk away, then turned back around. "I think I've got a copy in my bag. I'd be happy to lend it to you if you want to read it." He melted back into the crowd.

Borges shrugged and rolled his sightless eyes toward the ceiling. "What is that idiot talking about?"

Unfortunately I knew exactly what he was talking about. With Borges's encouragement, I had written up some of our first adventures in detection and submitted them to *True Crime* magazine, which published them in its next issue. A few months later a pastiche of the stories appeared in the *Revue des Deux Mondes,* authored by a professor who called himself R. Avallané (a pseudonym I'd just now understood), in which Borges (renamed Porges) is portrayed as a self-important fool playing at being a detective, a literary Inspector Clouseau whose investigations and solutions are palpably absurd.

It was this parody that Moreau handed to Borges after the conference adjourned. I had read it when it appeared and I dreaded describing it to Borges, or even worse, reading it to him. Luckily Moreau came to the rescue by quickly changing the subject. "Will I see you at the Dukes this evening?" he asked Borges with an ironic smile. "You'll love Alexandra. She's a great admirer of your work—and an extraordinarily beautiful woman. Scandinavian, needless to say."

You might have thought that Borges, being blind, would be immune to the charms of feminine beauty. But the truth is that he had a weakness for beautiful women, especially of the Scandinavian type. When the conference had ended and we'd trekked back to the hotel in the pouring rain to fetch his luggage (luckily we'd both worn raincoats), he insisted on stopping at the barber shop in the lobby for a shave. He then spent half an hour combing his thin halo of gray hair, muttering all the while about the woman who would be our hostess that weekend. "Alexandra... named after the conqueror of the world... long-limbed, buxom, mysterious..."

"Have you ever met Mrs. Duke?" I asked him.

"Not in person, but I spoke with her on the telephone. She has the voice of an astonishingly beautiful woman."

I retrieved my car from the hotel garage and somehow managed to maneuver him into it. As we drove out to Lincoln where the Dukes' estate was located, the subject of the detective parody came up only briefly. "I had not intended for you to write up any more cases beyond the ones we've already published," Borges said, "but I can see now that it will be necessary. The false narrative authored by Professor Avallané cannot stand uncontradicted."

"First we'll have to solve another mystery," I pointed out. "And before we can do that, there will have to be another murder."

"For which," he chuckled, "what could be a better setting than a weekend house party in the country, attended by Philippe Moreau?"

That sent a small shiver down my spine. I'd been surprised that Borges seemed already familiar with the parody published in the *Revue des Deux Mondes,* contrary to the reaction he'd shown to Moreau. Could the Frenchman's suspicions be correct? Could it be that Borges, like Cervantes, had written the parody himself—and then pretended to be outraged by it?

How very Borgesian!

2.

The Dukes inhabited a Victorian mansion in the posh, horsy suburb of Lincoln, a stone's throw from Walden Pond (though I would have been surprised if Maximilian Duke had ever heard of Henry David Thoreau). Duke had cleared most of the trees from the property and put in a parking lot, which, when we arrived, was already filled with expensive cars. We pulled on our raincoats and arduously made our way toward the house.

A lovely young lady in the livery of a maid greeted us at the front door and led us through a foyer into a crowded, noisy room she called the parlor. Ordinarily I would steer

Borges toward the nearest empty chair, but he insisted on meeting our hostess before we sat down. Alexandra Duke stood surrounded by guests beside a moveable bar—at least her voice (which Borges had described as the voice of a Scandinavian angel) seemed to be coming from there. My view was blocked by the throng of guests; then for an instant the crowd parted and I glimpsed an astonishing sight. I had expected a tall, strapping Valkyrie who looked like the St. Pauli girl with gossamer wings. But the Alexandra Duke I saw could hardly have been more different. She stood under five feet tall and had coal-black hair, dark, beetling brows and a remarkably flat chest. Her thin lips, beneath a light mustache, curled around a mouthful of ill-sorted teeth. Thomas Hobbes, if pressed on the point, might have described her as nasty, brutish and short.

Borges, however, as a blind man and a Platonist, perceived nothing but the heavenly music of her voice. "Ah, the incomparable Alexandra!" he exclaimed, tapping the floor with his walking stick as we inched forward. "Can there be another woman who matches her beauty?"

This drew a guffaw from a smirking young man with long hair, sideburns and a hipster goatee (this was the seventies, remember) who introduced himself as Jackson Duke, Maximilian Duke's son by a long-previous marriage. Noting the red-tipped cane, he foolishly tried to tell Borges the truth about his stepmother. "There's something somebody ought to tell you, man," he said in a low voice, "seeing as how you're blind. Alexandra isn't exactly beautiful. In fact, she's—"

I shot him a warning glance.

"She's what?" Borges probed.

"Sort of... plain."

That was a lie—she was about as plain as a pepperoni, sausage and anchovy pizza—but I acknowledged it with an appreciative wink.

Borges smelled a rat. "Plain?" he exclaimed. "Surely you don't expect me to believe that! If Sancho Panza had claimed that Dulcinea was plain, would even a madman like Don Quixote have credited such a calumny? Is there no such thing as chivalry in the modern world?"

"Only madness," I muttered.

"Like most men today, you are beguiled by the world of appearances."

"Far out, man!" Jackson cried out approvingly.

Obviously baffled by that expression, Borges went on: "Only a blind man can see the essence of things."

"Heavy!" Jackson said, and Borges's bafflement deepened. But before the young man could elaborate, he was shoved aside by Philippe Moreau, gimlet eyes glistening, a Gauloise dangling from his lips. "Ah, Borges!" he rasped. "So glad you could make it. Have you met the incomparable Alexandra?"

"Only from afar," Borges said. "I can hear her voice, but we have not yet come face to face."

"I'll take care of that," Moreau said, hooking his grip around Borges's elbow. "Let me introduce you."

I recalled that Moreau had described Alexandra as extraordinarily beautiful. Was he as blind as Borges, or had some magical mist blinded him to what every other man could see? Either that, I thought, or he was laughing at Borges, which did not bode well for the weekend.

The next patch of territory between Borges and his Dulcinea was not won without a struggle. A middle-aged couple with identical eyeglasses and matching smiles, the woman topped with orange-reddish hair, the man sallow-faced and almost bald, both of them balancing tiny plates of hors d'oeuvres and glasses of white wine, lurched in front of Moreau and blocked his way. "Arthur R. Koenig, Robert Thayer Batchellor Professor of International Jurisprudence at Harvard Law School," the man announced, gnawing a shrimp which he held on a toothpick. He wore a three-piece tweed suit with a crimson club tie. "And you are?"

Moreau was momentarily nonplussed. Apparently he assumed that the professor would recognize him. "I'm... Philippe Moreau," he finally said, trying to slip away. "You've probably heard of me. And this gentleman is Jorge Luis Borges."

Professor Koenig peered into Borges's empty gaze. "I remember you from when you lectured at Harvard a few years ago," he said. "You're from Buenos Aires, aren't you? I once stayed at the Hotel Crillon—three nights, in October of 1959. Hand-size Ivory soap was all they had in my room. Very brittle now; it has to be kept in a special controlled environment."

"My husband drafted the Argentine constitution," his wife said with a fanatical gleam in her eyes.

"Which is not worth the paper it's printed on," Borges grunted.

"Few of them are," the professor admitted with a smile. "At any rate, the real reason I went there was for the soap."

Before any explanation of this bizarre disclosure could be offered, a younger and much more attractive woman pushed her way in front of Professor Koenig and threw her arms around Moreau. "Philippe!" she gushed. "So good to see you! I hope we can catch up. Will you be staying the night?"

"Regrettably not," Moreau said, kissing her lightly on the cheek. "My wife is ill and I must hurry back to our hotel." He pivoted toward Borges and me. "I'd like you to meet Jorge Luis Borges and his assistant Nick Martin. This is Helen Rizzoli."

"So wonderful to meet you!" She squeezed my hand as if she meant it, but I knew better than to believe that. She was the reporter we'd seen on the TV news that afternoon—the station, I later learned, was part of Maximilian Duke's media empire—who had amused us with her account of the ironic twist of fate on the Massachusetts Turnpike. She wore a low-cut evening dress, gold Egyptian-themed earrings, and a magenta scarf around her long, shapely neck. Beside her hovered a dark, nondescript man in a dark, nondescript suit—she introduced him as her husband Dennis—who might have been a lawyer, an accountant or a Mafia hitman. In an ironic twist of fate, he was not the type who appreciated a French postmodernist kissing his wife.

"Let's go, honey," he said, tipping an unfriendly glance toward Moreau. "I need a drink."

Moreau drew Borges closer to the bar, where Alexandra Duke's siren song beckoned over the hubbub, leaving me in the clutches of Professor Koenig and his fanatical wife. "Arthur has drafted the constitutions of over a hundred and fifty countries," she gushed, "each of which he visited in person. In fact he's the only man in history who has visited every country in the United Nations General Assembly."

Professor Koenig nodded modestly to confirm this astonishing claim.

"In his travels—to document this achievement—he has collected small complimentary soap bars from over a thousand hotels, at least one in each country, with the name of the hotel printed on the packaging and the date of his visit handwritten in ink."

"And in case you're wondering," the professor interjected, "our estate plan provides that the entire collection—which occupies three hundred linear feet of shelf space in our home in Cambridge—will, upon our demise, be donated to the Ripley's Believe-It-Or-Not Museum in St. Augustine, Florida. The museum has gratefully accepted the donation, and of course an appropriate tax write-off will be applied."

"It's hard to imagine what such a collection must be worth," I said.

"Well into seven figures," he confided in a low voice, and he and his wife melted into the crowd.

The pretty maid appeared beside me with a tray of hors d'oeuvres: breaded shrimp, stuffed grape leaves, pigs-in-a-blanket. I impaled one of each with a toothpick and transferred them to a cocktail napkin. "Would you like a plate?" she asked. She had soft pink cheeks and cornflower blue eyes and she spoke with an accent that might have been French. In another lifetime I might have fallen in love with her.

"No time for that," I said as I wolfed down the hors d'oeuvres. "Thanks anyway."

She smiled and I asked her name.

"Geneviève."

"Are you a member of the family?"

She blushed as she shook her head. Out of modesty? Embarrassment at her lowly status? Or had I touched on some secret I shouldn't have known anything about?

"Just the maid." She bowed slightly and turned to leave. "If you'll excuse me, please."

I took this opportunity to rid myself of Borges's dripping raincoat, which he had left draped over my arm, as well as my own. Wandering back into the foyer, I found a walk-in coat closet behind a small door. As I arranged the raincoats on hangers, I heard voices coming through the wall. Bending closer, I discovered a narrow opening behind the coats, through which an unseen observer could peer into the parlor and hear what was being said with remarkable clarity. There was Helen Rizzoli, in newscaster mode, delivering a staccato account of a recent shooting in South Boston as her brooding husband stood guard with jealous eyes. Professor Koenig entertaining a Beacon Hill matron with his adventures in soap collecting. Philippe Moreau almost invisible behind a cloud of cigarette smoke, lost in postmodern thought. Jackson Duke, at the bar, drinking straight gin as he chatted with the bartender, a young man about his own age who had the dazed, bleached-out appearance of someone who'd spent too much time in the sun. I later learned that this was Trevor, who until recently had been the pool boy. Where, I wondered, was the great man himself? Where was Maximilian Duke?

Back in the parlor, I found Borges firmly in Alexandra Duke's grip, enthralled by her beauty as he envisioned it in his Platonic imagination. Taking his hand, she led him to a cluster of chairs along the wall and the two of them sat together, Borges tall and dignified, Alexandra small, dark, almost feral in appearance. Yet still her voice—and the personality it embodied—was magnificent. I grabbed a drink from the table and took a seat just close enough to hear the conversation.

"I must apologize for my husband's unsociable behavior," she was saying. "He's been out of sorts lately over an absurd obsession with his horoscope."

"His horoscope?"

"He's always been exceedingly superstitious. In his early years he had a run of impossibly good luck, as if he was fated to be rich and famous. Then about two weeks ago we had an astrologer as a house guest, who insisted on casting his horoscope. The horoscope warned—no, decreed—that he would suffer death at an early age in a body of water. His famous luck has turned on itself."

"As it does for all men sooner or later."

"He immediately started thinking of ways to save himself," she went on. "He resolved to stay off ships, even bridges, sell our beach house, give up sailing, swimming and fishing—in short, to avoid bodies of water at all cost." She grimaced with a pained expression. "He even drained the pool and fired the pool boy."

"I hope those measures succeed," Borges said, "but frankly they never do. In the literature—I'm referring, of course, to Arabian tales and the Norse sagas—even the gods lack the power to alter a person's fate."

At this moment Maximilian Duke lurched up beside us. "It wasn't fate that made me rich and famous," he growled, balancing a martini he'd carried with him from the bar. He was a tall, ruddy, imposing man, definitely the captain-of-industry type who could make the earth shake by wiggling his little finger. "It was my innate abilities, my capacity for hard work. My ambition, my *instinct for success,* as *Time* magazine put it. Luck had nothing to do with it."

"Professor Borges," Alexandra said, "this is my husband, Max. I hope you'll forgive his rudeness. He isn't fit to talk to until he has a few martinis under his belt."

"Don't confuse luck with fate," Borges said, turning toward Duke. "All the luck in the world won't keep you from meeting your fate."

"My fate?"

Borges bowed his head slightly. "The fate of every man—and every woman. We all share the same fate."

Duke's color rose to a fiery red. "You're talking about dying, aren't you? Well, I'll tell you something, professor. I know I'm going to die someday, but it won't be anytime soon and it won't be in a body of water. I'll see to that."

"Perhaps in something smaller," Alexandra smiled. "Like a martini glass?"

Duke caught his son Jackson's eye and lumbered away. I watched the two of them snag Professor Koenig and Helen's husband Dennis into an impromptu meeting that took them through a pair of French doors onto a sun porch furnished with a table and chairs and a lot of potted plants. Dennis—who, I later learned, was an investigative reporter at Duke's Boston newspaper—closed the French doors behind them to block their voices. Through the mullioned panes I could see Dennis setting a leather attaché case on the table and opening it to show Professor Koenig whatever was inside it. The color drained from the professor's face and he sat down as Duke raised his voice and shook his finger at him—could this have been over some bar of Ivory soap he'd filched from a hotel room?—while the others crowded around and watched him squirm.

Alexandra fell discreetly silent as this silent drama unfolded and I described it to Borges. "I know what you're thinking," she said. "Max is an insufferable bully. I'm last in a long line of wives who eventually couldn't stand him."

He sounded a note of hope. "Perhaps not the last."

"If another woman wanted him," she smiled, "I wouldn't stand in her way. Except for his money, of course."

The French doors flew open and the four men burst out—Duke, his son Jackson, Professor Koenig, and Dennis Rizzoli clinging grimly to his attaché case as if it contained the nuclear attack codes, still arguing, only now Duke and Jackson were arguing with each other.

"I had my building in the bag," Duke said as the professor scurried away, "and you had to open your stupid mouth and spout your hippie politics."

"All I said was—"

"I know what you said."

—"that law is just another tool of oppression."

"You're going to find out about tools of oppression. Picks and shovels, hammers, wrenches—because that's what you'll be using the rest of your life. Unless you'd prefer to serve hamburgers at McDonalds."

Jackson tried to block his father's way, gripping his forearms to hold him back. "You're not cutting me off, are you?"

"Damn straight I'm cutting you off!" Duke tore off Jackson's grip and pushed him aside. "Just as soon as I can get my lawyer on the phone. It'll take him about two minutes to scratch your name out of the will and write in the name of my horse. Even at three hundred dollars an hour, that two minutes will be the best money I ever spent."

Throughout this confrontation Dennis had stood behind Duke holding his attaché case. When he noticed me staring at them, he said, "Come on, Max. Let's not make a scene in front of your guests."

Dennis and Duke broke away and disappeared into the foyer. Jackson, his color high, gasping to catch his breath, stumbled over to the bar and poured himself a tall class of whisky. The sun-dazed bartender had vanished.

Borges had heard it all. "What was that all about?" he asked me, and I did my best to explain. Something had gone on behind those French doors that pitted Duke and his son against Professor Koenig (and I suspected it had little to do with bars of soap or the constitutions of obscure countries in the United Nations General Assembly), and Jackson had spoiled the game by voicing inane political opinions that offended the professor.

"Leading Duke to threaten to cut him out of his will," Borges nodded. "I also heard something about a building. Did you catch that?"

"I did but I have no idea what it meant."

Suddenly Moreau loomed in front of us, waving an empty glass. "Has anyone seen the bartender?" he called out. "I could use a drink over here."

"It's self-service around here," Jackson told him with a smirk. "You ought to know about that."

"Where did Trevor go?"

"I saw him leave with Alexandra, if you really want to know."

"That mindless, sunburned lump of tumescent flesh!" Moreau spat.

"What are you suggesting?" Borges cried out.

"Mind your own business, Mister Magoo."

Fortunately Borges missed the allusion. He gripped his walking stick and pounded it on the rug. "I will not hear Alexandra's honor besmirched in her own home. If you continue I will insist that we settle this outside."

Moreau laughed in his face and stalked away.

"Right on, brother!" Jackson cheered. "I'd like to see you give that French phony a good whack with your cane. You see, he and Alexandra—"

"I will not hear any more insults to my Dulcinea or it will be you who feels the brunt of my wrath."

Craving another pig-in-a-blanket, I went searching for Geneviève and found her standing apart from the crowd with her hors d'oeuvres tray empty. Her lovely blue eyes narrowed when she saw me coming, as if I brought back unpleasant memories. "I'm sorry if I embarrassed you," I said, "asking if you were a member of the family."

She seemed amused by my apology. "If you knew this family"—something hard and unforgiving lurked behind her sweet smile—"you'd know why I was embarrassed."

I could only imagine. "What's the story on Jackson?"

"The story?" she laughed. "That would be something like *Easy Rider* meets *The Paper Chase*. He's a spoiled, drugged-out rich kid who drives a Porsche and wrings his hands over the plight of the masses. He's already squandered a small fortune on yoga instructors, meditation gurus and criminal defense lawyers and now he wants to go to Harvard Law School, if he doesn't get locked up first."

"Locked up? You mean jail?"

She tapped her forehead. "Looney bin."

"You seem to know a lot about what's going on around here."

"A little too much." She beckoned with a barely perceptible nod and I followed her into the kitchen, where she set about frying up another batch of breaded shrimp. The door to a pantry stood ajar, through which the unmistakable sound of sighs and heavy breathing could be heard. I peeked inside and found our diminutive hostess Alexandra on a footstool making out with Trevor, the beefy bartender and ex-pool boy, who had his hand under her dress. When Alexandra saw me she calmly reached out and shut the door in my face. I turned around to find Geneviève grinning, not the least bit surprised or embarrassed.

"Quite a little Peyton Place you're running here."

"It's like this," she said. "Alexandra is getting it on with Trevor, Max is sleeping with Helen—"

"The news anchor?"

She nodded. "And Jackson has tried to rape me on numerous occasions."

The last part surprised me. "Jackson? He hardly seems like the violent type."

"In Mexico he shoved a man into an empty swimming pool and broke his neck. Max had to fly down there and bribe his way out of jail—he was so mad he threatened to disinherit him. That was six months ago. Now Jackson claims he's mended his ways—every day I hear him pleading with his father not to cut him out of his will."

"What does Max say?"

"He says he'll leave him in if he can get into Harvard Law School."

I had to laugh. "There's no way Harvard's going to let that doofus in."

"I wouldn't be so sure. Why do you think that professor's here?"

"The soap professor?"

She nodded. "They've got something on him. They're leaning on him to let Jackson in."

I recalled the heated argument I'd witnessed through the French doors and the confrontation between Duke and Jackson that followed. "There must be more to it than that," I said. "Did you see them arguing on the sun porch? It couldn't have been about getting one more rich kid into Harvard."

"I wouldn't know," she said. "I do know that Max is planning to visit Helen tonight in Trevor's cabana at 1:00 am."

"A threesome?"

She shook her head. "Trevor's sleeping in the house. Probably not with Alexandra, if Philippe Moreau is here."

"She's sleeping with Moreau too?" That would explain Moreau's low opinion of the ex-pool boy.

Geneviève nodded demurely. "I'm afraid so."

"How do you know all this, right down to the schedule?"

"You mean about Max and Helen? Before you got here the professor's wife followed me in here to get some more shrimp—the same way you just did—and Max was making out with Helen in the pantry, just like Alexandra and Trevor are doing now." When she glanced toward the pantry I couldn't help but admire her dimpled cheek and her cornflower-blue eyes. "Naturally we could hear everything that went on. I'll tell you one more thing and then I've got to stop. Helen told Max she was planning to slip Dennis some valium before he goes to bed so he won't wake up when she goes over to the cabana."

"You're making that up."

"If you don't believe me, ask Mrs. Koenig."

I had no reason to doubt any of this, though I did wonder how Geneviève fit in. Who was she sleeping with? "Like I said, quite a little Peyton Place. Why do you stick around?"

"I have visa issues which only Max can resolve. He's my employer. And in case you're wondering"—she favored me with a sly smile—"I'm not sleeping with him."

The crowd thinned out until the only remaining guests were those invited to stay for dinner. When Geneviève announced that dinner was being served in the formal dining room, Alexandra took Borges's hand and escorted him to his place at the table. I left them alone together while I slipped outside for a breath of fresh air. A sliding door led out from the kitchen to a wide patio, which extended back to a large swimming pool bookended by red-roofed cabanas at either end. There was no water in the pool—I recalled Alexandra having said that Max had drained it. The rain had stopped and it was a beautiful September evening, with a light mist drifting over the patio and the empty pool toward a wooded area farther back. Potted palms and flowering hibiscus plants lent the scene an exotic, almost Middle Eastern flavor. As I later learned, the cabana on the right would be the sleeping quarters of Helen Rizzoli and her husband Dennis. The one on the left (recently vacated by Trevor) was where the assignation between Helen and Maximilian Duke had been arranged.

Dinner was uncomfortable, to say the least. Geneviève and Trevor did their best to keep us supplied with food and drink, and what we had was very good. Duke boasted about his successes and ridiculed Jackson about his failures, ignored Alexandra, flirted with Helen, scowled at Trevor. Everybody seemed afraid of him, especially Trevor, who skirted around him like a dangerous animal as he poured the wine. Alexandra tried to keep the conversation going, feigning interest in Moreau's literary theories, Helen's name dropping, and the professor's soap collection. Dennis and Helen ignored each other, as married couples usually do on such occasions, and everybody ignored me. Borges waited until all had exhausted their pet topics, and then he launched into a monologue about the second century heresiarch Basilides the False, who taught that human beings were created out of base matter by an abominable demiurge. Several guests excused themselves and left the table before the coffee and dessert were served.

3.

Borges and I, when we worked together on a case, always enjoyed sipping a nightcap before going to bed. Our bedroom—Borges had insisted that we share a room, owing to his disability—contained a wet bar and a pair of wing chairs such as you might find in a gentleman's club. I poured a whisky for Borges—Chivas Regal, not bad—and a glass of port for myself, and we leaned back in our chairs listening to the wall clock tick off the seconds left in the universe. That (or it might have been the drinks) gave us the illusion that we could sit there counting them forever.

"I made an interesting discovery when I hung up your raincoat," I told Borges as I savored my first sip of port. "In the back of the coat closet there's a row of peep holes that look into the parlor. Someone could stand there and spy on whoever is in the parlor."

"A servant, perhaps?"

"Or a family member. There's a lot more going on in this house than meets the eye."

"There always is, especially to an eye like mine."

"Sorry. I shouldn't have used that expression."

"Not at all," he chuckled. "I still have a mind's eye which is far superior to the ordinary ones. It can see past the veil of appearances into the essence of things."

My own perceptions being more mundane, I filled him in on the gossip I'd heard from the maid (minus her revelations about Alexandra's extracurricular sex life). "Apparently our friend Jackson has a violent streak," I said. "I heard that from the maid, who says he tried to rape her more than once."

"Hard to believe."

I took another sip of port and let it trickle over my tongue. "She also says he got in big trouble down in

Mexico—threw a man into an empty swimming pool and broke his neck—and his father had to bribe his way out of jail, and then threatened to disinherit him. Now Duke is saying he'll only keep him in his will if he can get into Harvard Law School."

"That's absurd," Borges said.

"It would explain that scene on the sun porch with Professor Koenig."

"No, it wouldn't. There must be something else going on."

"Maybe so. Would you like another whisky?"

He held up his glass and I refilled it from the bottle. He drank it neat. "There's another thing the maid told me," I said. "I guess this should come as no surprise. Max Duke is carrying on an affair with Helen Rizzoli."

"The TV newscaster who likes ironic twists of fate?"

"The same. She's meeting him in the pool boy's cabana at 1:00 a.m. And get this—planning to drug her husband with valium so he won't notice her slipping out and back into their room."

Borges laughed and almost choked on his whisky. "What is that if it isn't tempting fate?"

"Tempting fate to do what?"

"To exact its price, as fate always does."

The two of us sat quietly for a moment, enveloped in the warm glow of the alcohol. The exactions of fate were the farthest thing from my mind. "You realize that these weekend house parties are the most common venue for murders," Borges said "Usually at night when the guests are supposed to be asleep. I've read about dozens of such cases. In most of them the murderer has plotted out the crime in advance, as if he were writing a detective story. The victim, the murder weapon, the suspects, even the detective and his solution—all have been predetermined, as if by the hand of fate."

"Even the detective's solution?" I asked incredulously.

"Ah, yes. You must remember that in the murderer's mind the detective is not fated to solve the crime. Or if he does, he will arrive at a false solution, contrived by the murderer."

All this talk about fate was making me uncomfortable. "It's so easy to slip into talking about fate as if it really existed," I said.

"Of course it exists," Borges smiled, swirling the whisky in his glass, "though we don't call it fate anymore. We call it causation." He lifted the glass and drained it in one long swallow. "Which, as Hume took pains to show, is equally a matter of superstition, or 'custom' as he called it. But what a custom! It dominates our lives. Not supernatural, but immanent in the material world—causation is to us what fate was to the ancients: inexorable, implacable, inescapable. And the detective's job is to trace it back, follow its every turn until he can see the entire chain of events that led to the crime. Motive, means and opportunity—those are the three Norns that shape the course of the criminal's destiny."

I mulled what he had said as I sipped my port. There was a fallacy in his logic, but I couldn't put my finger on it. "In theory, then," I said, "since that chain of events is so ineluctable, you should be able to trace it forward as well as back. You should be able to predict the future with the same assurance that you can reconstruct the past."

"Time is the medium of fate," he said. "It winds its way forward through the labyrinth of infinite possibilities, each step a bifurcation that forecloses every route except the one chosen. Looking backward, it's easy to see the steps that were taken and how they led to one another. But to look forward—you'd have to be a prophet or a soothsayer to see the steps that *will* be taken."

He held up his glass and I obliged him with another shot of Chivas. While I was at it I topped off my port, and then sat down. "Why not give it a try?"

He smiled broadly. "Based on my observations of the people in this house, I think I can venture a few predictions."

"First tell me about our host."

Setting his glass down, he leaned back in his chair and tilted his sightless gaze upward as if opening his mind to hidden forces. "Mr. Duke will trigger his own doom by trying to avoid it," he said. "Many an arrogant fool has done so—in fact, in certain Arabian tales and Norse sagas, it's the fate specially reserved for arrogant fools."

"Will he die in a body of water?"

"Most likely, if water has anything to say about it."

"What will become of Jackson?"

"Like all dim-witted sons of powerful men, he will vanish before the truth about him can be known."

"And the others?"

"Professor Koenig, I can confidently assert, will end his career in disgrace. The newscaster Helen Rizzoli will suffer an ironic twist of fate, probably at the hands of her cuckolded husband. And our friend Philippe Moreau—if I were one of the three fates, I would weave for him an eternity of torment rivaling those of Tantalus and Sisyphus. He will be undone by the objective reality which he pretends does not exist."

There was one person—to Borges the most important—whose fate had gone unmentioned. "I hesitate to ask," I said, "but what about Alexandra?"

"Ah, Alexandra!" The utterance of her name brought him upright, shaking himself out of his reverie. "Alexandra will suffer the fate of all beautiful women, which is to be loved by fools like me."

I collected our glasses and set them in the small sink, then helped Borges undress and get ready for bed. The clock had ticked past midnight and the sensible world had receded into darkness and silence. I had one last question before I turned off the lights. "Do you expect anyone to be murdered tonight?"

"Absolutely."

"Who are you rooting for?"

He allowed himself a brief, sardonic smile. "Philippe Moreau, obviously. I would do anything in my power to ensure that he is the victim. Short of killing him, of course."

"He's not even here," I pointed out. "He went back to his hotel to be with his wife."

"A banal plot twist. He could be anywhere."

4.

When I awoke, Borges sat on the edge of his bed, dressed in a conservative gray suit. His thin gray hair was neatly combed, his tasteful blue necktie tied in a Windsor knot. Apparently he could find his way around in the visible world quite capably when he wanted to. I quickly dressed and spruced myself up, reassuring Borges, who was anxious about his appearance in the company of Alexandra, that he looked the perfect gentleman.

As I guided him downstairs we heard what I took for the screeching of a blue jay—in fact it was a clock on the kitchen wall that emitted bird calls on the hour instead of gongs. We were just in time for breakfast, which was to be served on the patio at nine o'clock, at a wide round table between the house and the pool. Borges's disappointment was palpable when he smelled the odor of a Gauloise souring the air. Moreau was not dead, as he had hoped, but seated at the table, lecturing Alexandra on the correct method of poaching an egg as elucidated by Lacan and Derrida. I led Borges to his seat and carried our plates to the buffet, where I filled them with eggs benedict, sausage and Danish pastries. Geneviève and Trevor scurried in and out of the kitchen to replenish the buffet and keep the guests well-supplied with coffee and juices.

None of the other guests—Professor and Mrs. Koenig, Dennis and Helen Rizzoli—seemed especially happy to be there. Helen's puffy hair had detumesced into a frayed rat's nest and her makeup had run off in the night. Dennis was so hung over he had to struggle to keep his eyes open. The professor and his wife perched on the edges of their chairs, nibbling like chipmunks. They looked like they were counting the minutes until they could scurry away. Jackson, his hair pulled back into a ponytail, glared at the others as if he wished they would all go home.

"How is your wife?" Borges asked Moreau, probably so he would stop talking to Alexandra.

"Much better, thank you. She slept in so I decided to join you for breakfast."

"At my invitation," Alexandra smiled. "Philippe is always welcome here."

"He certainly is," Jackson said, arching his eyebrows. An empty seat separated him from Alexandra, who gripped her fork as if she meant to spear him with it. "I wonder where my father is," he said.

"Up in his room," she suggested, "cutting you out of his will."

"If he does, I'll have Professor Koenig to thank for that."

"Now see here," the professor objected. "I won't be intimidated by—"

"Come on, children!" Alexandra said, forcing a laugh. "I'm sure everything we've said was all in good fun. Geneviève, why don't you run upstairs and tell Mr. Duke that we're down here waiting for him."

The maid left and came back a few minutes later. "He's not up there."

"Then please go out and see if he's in the cabana," Alexandra said. She explained to the rest of us: "Sometimes he sleeps out there."

We heard a muffled scream and Geneviève came running back. "Max—Mr. Duke—is in the pool!"

"What on earth is he doing there?"

"I think he's dead."

We all jumped up and rushed to the pool, including Borges, who stumbled along clinging to my arm. Maximilian Duke, in a terry cloth bathrobe and plastic flip-flops, lay crumpled on the dry cement, twelve feet down. His neck was bent at an unnatural angle and dark blood trailed out of his mouth. His eyes were wide open.

I described what I saw to Borges. "Is he dead?" he asked.

"No question about it."

Jackson shrieked when he saw his father on the bottom of the pool. He vaulted down a ladder on the side and crouched over the body, but there was nothing he could do.

"Don't touch him!" someone called out—I think it was Trevor. "Somebody call the police."

Jackson stared up at us in wide-eyed terror, as if he thought the police would be coming for him. Then he stood up and paced around on the bottom of the pool, keeping his eyes down.

"What an ironic twist of fate!" said Helen, who seemed to keep a lookout for such things.

"His horoscope said he would die in a body of water, so he drained the pool. But it's still a body of water, isn't it?"

"Without that horoscope he'd still be alive," Dennis agreed. "A little wet, maybe, but still alive."

"No one could have prevented it," Alexandra said, her voice cracking.

"Except the one who cast the horoscope," Professor Koenig said, prompting some uncomfortable murmuring from the others.

"And the one who threw him in the pool," Borges added, and the murmuring stopped.

All eyes, none of them friendly, were on Borges. "Isn't it a little premature to be hurling accusations around?" Moreau asked him. "We don't know what happened."

"I have hurled no accusations. Anyone who thinks he has been accused, please speak up." The offer had no takers.

"I've got to sit down," Alexandra moaned, heading back to the table, where she collapsed sobbing with her head in her hands. The rest of us joined her there to wait for the police. All except Professor and Mrs. Koenig, who hovered beside the table, as if waiting for a chance to thank the hostess for a lovely time.

"Unfortunately," the professor said, "we must really be going. There's no reason—"

"Nobody leaves the patio," Borges declared in his most authoritative voice.

"And who are you to tell us that?" The professor's reedy voice dripped with scorn. "Aren't you a poet or something?"

"I am a poet, but I speak in my capacity as a detective."

"A detective? That's absurd!"

"I'm sure Mr. Moreau would agree with me."

Moreau drew a blue pack of Gauloises from his shirt pocket, shook out a cigarette and lighted it. "Of course Borges is right," he smiled. "Borges is always right. Everyone must stay until the police arrive."

"But is he a detective?"

"Yes, he absolutely is a detective. And you ignore him at your peril."

5.

Geneviève stepped into the kitchen to fetch another pot of coffee and then went around the table replenishing everyone's cup. Her face was as blank as the bare cement on the bottom of the pool. Trevor seemed unaffected by what he had seen. He brought a tray of pastries and set it in the center of the table. Alexandra continued to sob. Jackson came back from the pool and dropped into his seat at the table. He looked pale and apprehensive but seemed intent on regaining his composure.

Borges rapped his walking stick on the tile floor to command their attention. "Let's get started with the investigation," he said. "With apologies to Mr. Moreau, I'm going to assume that Mr. Duke was murdered. If the autopsy shows otherwise—which is highly unlikely—we will have spent an amusing half hour speculating over a crime that was never committed."

The professor, who had sat back down, popped up again like a lawyer objecting at a trial. "I'm not going to sit here and—"

"If you don't wish to participate," Borges cut him off, "you're not obliged to do so. Your refusal will be noted, however, and reported to the police. There are some people here who would undoubtedly prefer to resolve this matter before the police arrive. You may be one of them."

The professor fell back in his seat but kept his hands poised over the table in case he thought of further objections. "The first thing I would like to do," Borges said, "is to ask the maid a few questions."

"Yes," Geneviève said, padding up beside him.

"When you went upstairs to look for Mr. Duke—I assume you went to his private room?"

"Yes. Mr. and Mrs. Duke sleep in separate rooms."

"Are those rooms near each other?"

"No, they're on opposite ends of the house."

"You tapped on his door?"

"Yes. There was no answer."

"Did you open the door and look inside? Please tell us what you saw."

"The room looked like it always does. Mr. Duke wasn't there."

"Had the bed been slept in?"

"No, it didn't look like it had been."

Borges sat thinking for a moment. "Now I would ask you to walk past the end of the pool where Mr. Duke is lying, proceeding to the cabana—the one which until recently was occupied by the pool boy. Inspect the inside of it, without touching anything, including the door knob. Then come back and tell us what you found."

We sat in silence as Geneviève followed his instructions. When she came back she drew up beside Borges, who must have heard her approach. He gazed toward her with his glaucous eyes. "Did you look inside? What did you find?"

"Well, the bed in there has definitely been slept in. Or maybe slept isn't the right word."

"What else?"

"There's an empty wine bottle, a couple of half-empty wine glasses, an ashtray full of cigarette butts. The whole place is a mess."

"Did you ever go in there when it was occupied by the pool boy?"

"Sure. I'm responsible for cleaning all the rooms."

Trevor, standing by the buffet table, seemed to sense some danger in this line of questioning. "I always kept the place neat," he said, "and I don't smoke."

"So you've never found the room in such a state of disarray?" Borges asked Geneviève.

"Only once," she said, "a couple of weekends ago. We had another house party, with people staying overnight."

"I was serving," Trevor said, "so I slept inside, like I did last night."

"Who slept in the cabana?"

"Nobody, as far as I know."

"What about the other cabana? Did anyone sleep in there?"

"Helen and Dennis slept in there, like they did last night."

Helen stared straight ahead, her face hardened to the expressionless mask of a news anchor reporting an ironic twist of fate. She seemed to be waiting for a cue that never came. Her husband glared at Borges like an attack dog getting ready to leap. "On both occasions," he said, "we slept through the night. We didn't hear anybody falling into the pool or getting murdered."

"Had the pool been drained on that earlier weekend?"

"No, I don't believe it had been."

Alexandra spoke up for the first time. "Max drained it last week. On account of the horoscope."

"Just when did he get this horoscope?" Borges asked.

"I don't know. A couple of weeks ago."

"Where did it come from?"

"I think I mentioned," Alexandra said, "we had an astrologer as a house guest."

Borges folded his hands in front of him and leaned back as if lost in thought. "This horoscope predicted an early death in a body of water, so Mr. Duke drained the pool and fired the pool boy. But the pool boy is still here."

"I asked him to stay this weekend to help out," Alexandra said. "This is his last day."

Borges turned back to Geneviève. "Did you see anything else unusual in the cabana?"

Her blue eyes darted away like a frightened sparrow. "On the floor next to the bed there's a red scarf," she mumbled. "Magenta, really. A woman's scarf."

"Have you ever seen it before?"

"I'm not sure, but it might be the one Helen was wearing last night."

Helen, until then so wooden, came suddenly alive. "I'm sure it isn't," she said. "The one I had on last night is already packed in my suitcase."

"Excellent," Borges said. "That should be very easy for the police to confirm. If you want to have them getting involved in that aspect of the case."

He flicked his wrist and Geneviève bent closer as he whispered in her ear. She nodded and disappeared into the kitchen. "I like a little cream in my coffee," he explained, as if he'd sent her after it.

A nervous silence quivered over the table. They all tried to look carefree as they refrained from eating, drinking, talking or looking at each other. It was as if a shoe had dropped and each of them hoped nobody expected a second one. Then Alexandra broke the spell. "We might as well clear the air before the police get here," she said. "Max is dead and the rest of us know what went on in that cabana. I know, Geneviève and Trevor know, Dennis probably knows. I don't think we need to read about it in the papers."

"I didn't know anything about it," Jackson said, with a primness that was unbecoming in a man with a ponytail.

"No, you wouldn't."

"All right," Helen said, scowling. "It's my scarf and I was in the cabana with Max, just like I was two weekends ago. So what? Do you think these TV jobs grow on trees? Max wanted sex and I gave it to him."

They fidgeted, jiggled their spoons, shifted positions, and then the silence fell again. "And Dennis," Borges said, with surprising gentleness, "if I may ask, did you know about this?"

"Well," Dennis said, clinging to his last shred of dignity, "let's just say I wasn't surprised. I worked for Max too. I wasn't exactly his whore but it came pretty close to that."

"And I *was* his whore?" Helen bristled. "It was a casual affair, that's all, and you shared the benefits."

"Oh, I guess it's all right then."

"What I was doing for him wasn't half as bad as what you do every day."

"I'll vouch for that," the professor blurted.

This sudden intrusion brought everyone's head spinning around, including Mrs. Koenig's. The professor sat fiddling with the buttons on his tweed jacket, pretending to have no idea why they all stared at him.

Borges leaned forward and asked him, "Were you in the cabana too?"

"No, no. Of course not."

"Then what do you think Helen meant by saying what she did wasn't half as bad as what Dennis does?"

"I'd keep my mouth shut if I were you," Dennis warned him.

The professor glowered back at him defiantly. "I'm not afraid of you anymore."

At this point Jackson leaped into the argument. "I don't see that anything has changed. You'd still better make sure I get in."

"I've told you that's not going to happen."

"That's all we want now that my father's dead. Isn't it, Dennis?"

"Shut up, Jackson."

Borges hated being in the middle of an argument. He raised his cane and rapped it on the table—"Gentlemen!"— and they all turned toward him. "This is what I was talking about when I warned you about involving the police. Obviously there was some kind of extortion going on. I assume that the incriminating facts are contained in Dennis's leather attaché case."

The so-called gentlemen held their tongues but looked daggers at each other while Borges took a sip of his coffee. "I don't know if this has anything to do with the murder," he said. "If it doesn't, you'd better make a clean breast of it now. Extortion is a crime and the police would be very interested to hear about it."

The professor glanced at Dennis for permission to talk. "Max Duke was pressuring me into helping Jackson get into Harvard Law School," he said, "for which he is totally unqualified. That's all it was. There was no extortion."

"Professor Koenig," Borges said, "I was not born yesterday, or the day before yesterday, or the day before that. Please tell me the real reason. It was about a building, was it not?"

The professor twiddled his buttons for a moment and then brushed an imaginary speck of dust from his lapel. "He also wanted the law school to name a building after him.

Another ridiculous request which I rejected out of hand. Again, there was no extortion."

"He wanted Harvard to name a building after him?"

"Max had an inferiority complex," Alexandra said, "because he never finished college. He had offered Harvard a very generous donation on condition that they name a building after him, and they turned him down."

"Originally he wanted us to name the whole law school after him," the professor smiled. "Obviously that was a non-starter."

"But why did you turn him down on the building? Just because he never finished college?"

"No, because he was a crook. It wasn't extortion because I never agreed to any of his demands. Dennis can attest to that."

Dennis nodded grimly.

"Attempted extortion, then."

"No, it was just pressure. How could it have been extortion? They had nothing on me."

Borges snapped his fingers and Geneviève, who had been waiting in the kitchen, glided up beside him carrying Dennis's leather attaché case. A quick survey of the assembled company revealed differing degrees of shock, fear and consternation. The professor's eyes bulged as if he wished they could roll under the table.

"Maybe this will refresh your recollection," Borges said.

"Where did you get that?" Dennis demanded.

"I sent Geneviève up to the professor's room to look for it. Open it, my dear, and show us what's inside."

"You had no right to go in our room."

She set the briefcase on the table and snapped it open. They all knew what was in it, and of course Borges couldn't see anything. All I saw was a jumble of papers, photographs, diagrams, and the like.

"What is all this stuff?" I asked the professor.

"I can answer that," Dennis cut in. "He stole it from me."

"All right," Borges said. "Please tell us what it is."

"I'm an investigative reporter. At least that's what I used to be, when Max still put my work in the newspaper. In the last couple of years he gave me a different kind of assignment. I would conduct the usual investigation but my stories almost never got into print. Max used them to gain leverage over people he wanted something from."

"Blackmail," Borges said.

"He called it editorial discretion."

The professor had been eyeing the briefcase like a cat stalking a bird. Suddenly he lurched forward and tried to grab it, but Geneviève snatched it away and snapped it shut. She handed it to Borges, who wrapped his arms around it like a bag of groceries. "So what's in this briefcase?" he asked Dennis.

"What this material shows is that Professor Koenig is a charlatan," Dennis said. "His soap collection is mostly fake. He's never been to most of the countries it supposedly came from, and half of the hotels don't exist. Most of the constitutions he claims to have drafted were never adopted. When this is made public he will probably be fired by the law school and his lucrative deal with the Ripley's Believe-It-Or-Not Museum will go down the drain."

"It still sounds like blackmail to me," Borges said.

"Max Duke is dead. I'm going to use this material to write a long exposé to be published in the paper."

Professor Koenig was on his feet, then on top of Borges, trying to wrench the briefcase out of his embrace. I forced myself between them and Dennis pulled the professor away, forcing him back down into his seat. "Everything in that briefcase is mine!" the professor shouted, "and what isn't mine is libelous." He tried to push Dennis away. "You seem to forget that I'm a law professor. I know my rights."

Borges tightened his grip on the briefcase. "Both of you seem to forget that we're still investigating a murder. The fate of this briefcase will depend on how that investigation turns out."

6.

The clock in the kitchen twittered in the broken tones of a house sparrow. Ten o'clock, still early in what promised to be a long September day. The breakfast, considered as a social event, had been a spectacular flop. Most of the food on the table had barely been touched. The coffee was cold, the croissants stale, the fat on the sausages congealed. The buffet table swarmed with flies. The guests were anxious and weary, the hostess sobbing, and the host—whom they all would have preferred to forget about—lay dead on the bottom of the pool.

"I'd like to know what's taking the police so long," someone said.

"It's Saturday morning," someone else observed.

"How long did they say it would take them?" another person wondered.

No one ventured a response. A few minutes passed.

"Wait a minute," Dennis said. "Who called the police?"

Another long silence.

"Trevor, I thought you called them," Alexandra said.

"No, I just said somebody should call the police. I thought somebody else was going to do it."

"It's been an hour since we found the body," Helen said. "That doesn't look good."

"What, like we murdered him?" Trevor said.

"They don't need to know how long we sat here," Jackson said. "For all they know we came out here five minutes ago."

"Are you going to tell them that?" Helen asked.

"Why not?" the professor said. "It's not like we're hiding anything."

"Somebody is," Borges said. "Somebody at this table killed him."

Geneviève hurried into the kitchen and called the police. Everyone else sat grimly trying not to look at each other, disturbed by what Borges had said. One of them was a murderer. The only person smiling was Moreau, who had been uncharacteristically silent during the whole discussion. I'd noticed him running his hand through his hair, cleaning his eyeglasses with a napkin, and of course smoking the inevitable Gauloises. Smiling occasionally and shaking his head in silent amusement, as if he thought the whole exercise was much ado about nothing, a performance mounted by Borges for the benefit of Alexandra, his Dulcinea. I confess that the same thought had crossed my mind.

"I have to say, Borges, I think that's a completely unwarranted accusation," Moreau said, "even if it is directed to the group and not to any individual. We still don't know if Max was murdered. Why not let the police do their work before we start accusing each other?"

"I agree," Helen said. "Apparently I was the last one to see him alive. He was pretty drunk when I left him. How do we know he didn't stumble into the pool and break his neck?"

"Very well," Borges said. "Let's explore that possibility. Helen, I gather that you left the cabana before he did. What time was that?"

"I don't know. Probably about three."

"Do you know what Mr. Duke was planning to do?"

"Well, our understanding was that he would wait about fifteen minutes, in case anybody saw me leave the cabana. Dennis, Alexandra, or anybody else who might look out the window or happen to be out there."

"This was the practice you had established on previous occasions?"

"That's right."

"So you left and went back to your cabana. Was Dennis in there sleeping?"

"I think so. It has two single beds so I can't really say. I didn't look at him."

"Could you hear him breathing or snoring?"

"I don't remember. I assumed he was sound asleep."

"Was that because of the valium you had given him before he went to bed?"

Dennis glowered at Helen. "What the hell?"

"I don't know what he's talking about," she told him.

"Did you notice anything else when you went back to the cabana?" Borges asked.

"Yes, as a matter of fact I did. The door was ajar. Practically standing open. I didn't leave it like that."

"So maybe Dennis had gone out?

"I did not," Dennis said.

"He says he didn't," Helen said.

"But you can't say for sure that he didn't, can you?"

She looked worried, shaking her head, as she imagined the possibilities if her husband had left the cabana while she was in bed with Duke.

"Maybe he'd observed the pattern on previous occasions," Borges said, "and made a point of being out there, hiding in the trees or behind one of those big potted plants—after all, it was dark, wasn't it?—so he could wait for you to leave and then throw Mr. Duke into the pool when he left to go in the house. He certainly had a good motive. The oldest motive in the book."

"Listen, Mr. Poet," Dennis said. "You're not the police and we don't have to listen to you."

"No, but you should because if you're guilty, you and your wife need to get your lines straight before the police arrive. If you're not guilty, you should be wondering why the door was ajar when Helen returned to the cabana."

"Why?"

"Don't forget the attaché case that Geneviève found in the Koenigs' room. Somebody lifted it from your cabana— undoubtedly the professor or his wife. They intended to take it home with them this morning."

"You can't prove that," the professor said. "You're not even a proper detective."

"The proper detectives will be here soon. You can explain it all to them."

"The police will know a far-fetched story when they hear one."

"Yes, but in case they're wondering what emboldened you to sneak into the Rizzolis' cabana in the middle of the night to steal the briefcase, I think I'll be able to enlighten them with eyewitness testimony that your wife overheard Mr. Duke and Helen arranging their tryst, including the plan to drug Dennis with valium."

The professor and his wife were on their feet, ready to flee the table. Dennis and Helen stood up with the same intention. "Come on, Helen," Dennis said. "We don't have to obey this crackpot."

"Feel free to go. Only be aware that I will report your behavior to the police."

They hesitated ever so slightly. Then, to my surprise, it was Moreau who spoke up and he took Borges's side. "I think Borges's accusations are unwarranted," he said, "but before you run off there's something you should know. He's very well-known in police circles as a detective, and he's correct in saying that if you run away from him the police will scrutinize you very carefully."

The two couples exchanged glances and sat back down. "Go ahead," Dennis told Borges.

"Yes," the professor said. "Go on."

"Very well," Borges said. "We have identified four people—Helen, Dennis, Professor Koenig, and Mrs. Koenig—who were, or may have been, on the patio last night at the time Mr. Duke was killed. That gives us four suspects so far. Let's see if we can find the other two."

"The other two?" Jackson said. "What are you talking about?"

"There are always six suspects. Let me ask each of you: Is there anyone you suspect?"

Again Moreau spoke up, a little less reluctantly this time. "As I've said, we don't know if there's been a murder or not. But if there was, I think suspicion should fall on Trevor. He told me that Max had threatened to have him killed."

"Killed?" Borges asked. "He threatened to have you killed?"

Trevor nodded grimly. "He said if I didn't get out of here and stay away my life would be very short. Words to that effect."

"I'm afraid that's true," Alexandra said. "I heard him say it."

"That doesn't mean I killed him," Trevor said.

"Why was he threatening you?"

"We had personal differences."

"But if you feared for your life, why did you stay here?"

"I asked him to stay," Alexandra chimed in. "To serve at the party. Max agreed that he could stay through today."

"This was my last day," Trevor said. "Then I was getting out of here. I had no reason to kill him."

"Nevertheless," Borges said, "you are suspect No. 5. And now—"

Before he could say another word, we were besieged by a noisy contingent of the local constabulary—uniformed policemen, plainclothes policemen, forensics specialists, photographers, EMTs, ambulance drivers—who swarmed out of the kitchen and across the patio toward the pool, led by Geneviève, who had answered the front door. The officer in charge was Detective Sam Lurio, a tall, ungainly man with a hatchet face and a pair of glistening black eyes that had seen it all. He slouched beside the table inspecting us like suspects in a line-up. "Which one of you is the owner of this house?"

"I guess I am now," Alexandra said weakly. "My husband appears to be dead."

"And who are the rest of these people?"

"They're my guests. Except the two of them who are servants, and—"

"Excuse me, officer," the professor interrupted, rising. "My wife and I—"

"Sit down and listen up." Detective Lurio's gaze ranged over the table, singling each of us out in turn to register his conviction that we were guilty and would be dealt with accordingly. "Nobody's going anywhere. I don't care if you're late for an audience with the Pope. Stay put until I say you can leave. Is that clear?"

A uniformed cop stepped up beside him with a succinct report. "There's a stiff on the bottom of the pool."

He scowled at us in disgust and followed the cop back to the pool.

We sat in stunned silence for a moment before Borges spoke up. "As I was saying, we have yet to identify the sixth suspect. There is a person here—and several of you already know this—for whom the events of last night were not of an unprecedented nature. This is a person who had an exceptionally strong motive to eliminate Mr. Duke, and had the physical size and strength to do so. I should mention that a woman, such as Helen and Mrs. Koenig, no matter how strongly motivated, would never have attempted to kill him by pushing him into the pool. She would have poisoned him or stabbed him in his sleep. Even Professor Koenig—if you will excuse me—judging from the weakness of his handshake, would undoubtedly have found a less risky way to do the deed."

"I guess that points to me, then," Dennis said bitterly. "There's no evidence for it. It's pure speculation."

"Yes," Borges said. "There's another who fits the profile much better than you."

"You're talking about Trevor, aren't you?" Moreau crowed. "He's the brawniest one here and had the best motive."

"You son of a bitch!" Trevor said, lurching toward Moreau with his fists clenched.

Moreau stood up to him—he was surprisingly brawny himself. "And his violent tendencies are obvious. He's a menace to all of us."

Trevor stepped back. "You won't have to worry about me anymore, you French prick," he told Moreau. "I'll be out of here the minute they let me leave."

"You'd better be."

We were all surprised by the ferocity of the confrontation between Trevor and Moreau. Of course I knew what it was really about: both men had been enjoying Alexandra's favors—a fact I had withheld from Borges, to my later regret. A tragic ending could have been avoided if I'd told him the unpleasant truth about his Dulcinea.

But at the moment none of this had any apparent relevance to the case. "No," Borges went on, as if the confrontation had never happened, "Trevor was not the man I had in mind. I'm thinking of a man who, in Mexico last year, committed the very same crime—he threw a man into an empty swimming pool and broke his neck. I refer of course to Jackson Duke, who stood to lose a fortune if his father cut him out of his will, as he had recently threatened to do."

Jackson jumped up, his eyes wild with desperation. "I'm not going to listen to this!" He stood transfixed for a long moment as we all stared in judgment of him, then he darted toward the kitchen. Alexandra ran after him and they had a brief exchange in the kitchen, which none of us could hear. Then he turned and faced us one last time before disappearing into the house. "For the record, I didn't do it."

Again there was a long silence. We heard an engine roar in the driveway as his Porsche started up and drove away. No one chased after him or tried to prevent him from leaving. No one alerted the police, who crowded around the pool.

About ten minutes later Detective Lurio sauntered back to the table, where we sat in obedient immobility. He seemed pleased with himself, having inspected the corpse, the scene of the crime and the surrounding area, and given instructions to his team.

"Okay," he said, pulling up a chair—Jackson's chair, as it happened. "Now I'm going to question all of you until I get to the bottom of this."

"No need for that," Borges said. "The murder has been solved."

7.

Half an hour later we were all back where we'd started, in the parlor, under police guard. All except for Borges, whom Detective Lurio had held back on the patio for consultation. Apparently he was familiar with Borges's reputation. He listened eagerly as Borges described his investigation and the process of elimination which had revealed Jackson's guilt, quickly confirmed by his flight after the police arrived. At one point the detective had called Alexandra back out to the patio, and under questioning she admitted that Jackson had confessed to the crime during their brief conversation in the kitchen. The police sent out squad cars to try and find him, but so far, at least, he had slipped away.

Detective Lurio led Borges into the parlor and seated him in the empty chair beside me. "Jackson Duke has fled," he announced. "He confessed to his step-mother before he left, and we have no doubt that he's the perpetrator. We've put out an all-points bulletin and sooner or later we will find him. I want to thank Dr. Borges for his invaluable assistance in solving this crime. You are all free to go, but please leave your names and telephone numbers with the sergeant in case we need to contact you again."

The detective and the other officers left the room, and Borges turned his blind but withering gaze on Moreau. "I hope that when you return to France," he said, "you will confine yourself to postmodern theorizing, in which there is nothing either good or bad but thinking makes it so, and leave crime detection to those who understand it. And I trust that there will be no more spurious sequels to Nick Martin's admirable accounts of my exploits."

Moreau, at a loss for words, could only muster a sheepish smile. "Touché," he muttered, and padded out of the room. Alexandra stood up and followed him without a backward glance. The others—Helen and Dennis Rizzoli, Professor Koenig and his wife, the maid Geneviève, the pool boy

Trevor—all said their good-byes and filed out one after another, leaving Borges and me alone in the parlor.

"Well," I told Borges, "congratulations on another successful case. It was a classic country house mystery, and you handled it with your usual finesse."

"A mere bagatelle," he said with false modesty.

"You certainly set Moreau down a few notches. Although it must be sorely disappointing that he was neither the murderer nor the victim."

His smile was wide and terrifying. "I'm not done with him yet."

I laughed. "What else can you do?"

His sightless eyes had taken on the impenetrable glaze I'd seen so many times when he set his mind on some unutterable scheme. "I'll stay here while you go up and fetch the luggage. If you see Moreau out in the foyer, send him in."

I steadied myself and took a deep breath, then headed toward the foyer. When I opened the door I found Moreau on the threshold, chatting with Detective Lurio. "I was just going to tell Borges goodbye," he said, slipping past me into the parlor before I could stop him.

Borges's voice rang out: "Nick! While you're packing up, don't forget to grab my raincoat from the coat closet. You know the one I mean: the one with the holes in it."

That spun my mind around again. Holes? What was he talking about? There were no holes in his raincoat. And then it hit me. "Sure thing," I answered, as Moreau entered the parlor and shut the door behind him.

I smiled at Detective Lurio. "Wouldn't you like to be a fly on the wall for that conversation?"

He smiled back slyly.

"Follow me," I said.

In the coat closet there was just enough room for the two of us to watch through the peep holes as Moreau and Borges exchanged their last farewells. Their voices came through loud and clear.

"I hope you enjoyed your fifteen minutes of self-congratulation," Moreau was saying. "Unfortunately I must inform you that your triumph is a sham. Far from being a master-stroke of detection, as you portray it, this was another fiasco for the bumbling Detective Porges. I can't wait to write it up in the *Revue des Deux Mondes*."

"What are you talking about?"

"You didn't solve the murder."

"Nonsense."

"Let me explain." Moreau hooked his thumbs in his lapels and paced in front of Borges, cigarette dangling from his lips, like a hardboiled detective from a 1940s movie. "Your solution was based on Jackson's previous conviction for killing a man in almost identical circumstances. He had a compelling motive. He easily could have hidden near the cabana, overpowered Max when he came out and thrown him into the pool. The fact that he fled when confronted is highly incriminating."

"So far everything you've said confirms my solution," Borges said.

"They'll search for Jackson but they will never find him, because there's another fact you don't know, which detracts from the certainty of your solution: Jackson spent some hellish weeks in a Mexican prison. After his father bribed the warden to let him out, he swore to his family that he would never return to prison under any circumstances. He would do anything, he said, to avoid that fate. He even mentioned the possibility of driving his car off a cliff into the ocean. There are places along the coast north of here where he could do that and never be found. In other words, the fact of his flight proves nothing, other than his determination to stay out of prison. All that's left is the circumstance of his having committed a similar crime before. But of course that crime could have been duplicated by anyone who knew about it."

"That much is obvious. But who was the killer?"

Moreau lit another Gauloise and released a noxious plume of smoke into the air. "Well," he began, "let's assume, hypothetically, that there's another man (besides yourself) who is in love with Alexandra Duke—let's call him X—and this other man in fact has slept with her, and she has told him all about Jackson's troubles down in Mexico, not just the jail time but the crime that led to it, and the fact that Jackson swore he'd never go back to prison. And that she also told X that she would marry him if anything happened to her husband, and share with him all the riches she'd inherit in that event—even suggesting that a repetition of the Mexican dry swimming pool incident, this time breaking the neck of her husband, would ensure that the blame for such a crime would fall on Jackson and eliminate him as a competitor for Max's fortune."

"I must warn you not to slander Alexandra. You are out of bounds."

"Now let's say that Alexandra—and again all of this is hypothetical—paid an astrologer to cast a horoscope that would lead Max to drain the pool, knowing, from his past practice, that he would arrange a midnight tryst with Helen in the cabana on the weekend when X would be visiting, and when Jackson would be home begging not to be disinherited—"

Borges's fingers danced around the handle of his walking stick. "I will not sit here and listen to you insult the woman I love!"

"I'm only telling you what you already know, or could have known if you didn't blind yourself (pardon the expression) to the obvious facts. Alexandra was at least as guilty as X—more so, in fact, because she conceived the whole plan and lured him into carrying it out. But you are a gentleman and you must protect her at all costs."

Borges slammed the walking stick down on the floor and tried to stand up. "I insist that we settle this outside!"

"I know this is difficult for you, Borges," Moreau said, pushing down on his shoulders to keep him from standing up. "But imagine how difficult it must have been for X. Fortunately he was a postmodernist who had freed himself from the constraints of bourgeois morality. To satisfy Alexandra he had to make an existential leap, into crime, into murder itself. Even so he wouldn't have bent to her will except on one condition: it had to be a perfect crime, one which even Borges couldn't solve."

"You are the murderer."

"Remember, everything I said is hypothetical. But it casts you in bad light, doesn't it? You thought Nick Martin—or should I call him Sancho Panza?—would write up this case as another brilliant Borgesian triumph, but now you know that it was a failure by an incompetent impostor. Borges has indeed become Porges; I will write the definitive case report, showing you as the bumbler that you are. And your days of toying with the affections of Alexandra—your Dulcinea—are over. She will marry me and make me a rich man, while you, like Avellaneda's Quixote, will end your days in a lunatic asylum."

"You are the murderer," Borges repeated.

Moreau feigned incomprehension. "How could I be the murderer? I was twenty miles away, with my wife," he laughed.

"Like all false alibis, that can easily be disproved."

"You have no evidence."

Now it was Borges's turn to laugh. "Why concern ourselves with evidence when we have your confession?"

"My confession?" For the first time Moreau seemed unsure of himself. His eyes darted warily around the room. "Have you been recording this?"

"Of course not. I am a gentleman."

"Then no one has heard it but you. And who will believe a blind old megalomaniac who fancies himself a detective?"

Detective Lurio elbowed me aside and burrowed his way out of the closet through the hanging coats. I followed him through the foyer and into the parlor. He lurched across the room and snapped a pair of handcuffs on the astonished Frenchman.

"Philippe Moreau, I'm arresting you for the murder of Maximilian Duke."

Moreau knew better than to say anything that could be held against him. As Detective Lurio dragged him out of the room, he wheeled toward Borges for the last word on Dulcinea. "I lied to you about Alexandra, Borges," he said through his teeth. "She's not beautiful. Not even close."

8.

Again we sat alone in the parlor. The police had bundled Moreau into a squad car and driven him to the station to be booked for murder. Borges seemed depressed by the arrest, which should have delighted him. He closed his eyes, rubbed his forehead, moaned softly as if something was devouring him from the inside. I had never seen him like this.

"You knew it was Moreau all along, didn't you?" I asked him.

"I had my suspicions. The horoscope, the draining of the pool, the precise repetition of Jackson's crime—those had the hallmarks of free will, not of fate. Fate works in more devious ways."

"But in the end," I said, hoping to buck him up, "you did solve the crime."

He shook his head. "Only because that fool Moreau couldn't resist gloating about how he'd deceived me."

"But isn't that a time-honored tactic? Coaxing a confession out of a culprit who's eager to show how clever he is?"

We sat in silence while Borges mustered the courage to go on. "I made a mistake that no detective worthy of the name should ever make," he said. "I fell in love with someone who should have been a suspect—the prime suspect, as it turned out—and that twisted my whole perception of the case. Did Sherlock Holmes ever do that? No. Father Brown? Of course not. The only time I can recall it happening was in *Trent's Last Case*, with similarly disastrous results."

"Any man in the throes of love could have made that mistake," I said.

"It led me to overlook the solution that was staring me in the face. The solution that was so obvious that Moreau couldn't help taunting me with it."

"Which of course you knew he would do."

"It was his fate to be the author of his own downfall. I was the instrument of that fate."

"Maybe Moreau lied about Alexandra's involvement," I said.

"If anything he blinded himself to her machinations as much as I did." His sagging cheeks swayed as he shook his head. Closing his eyes, he bent forward and rested his forehead on his fingertips. "My Dulcinea a demon? I can't, I won't believe it!"

What do you say to a 75-year-old man pining after a woman half his age? Borges had only met Alexandra Duke the night before and he still had no idea what she looked like. Not that her appearance would have made any difference. It was the Platonic ideal which he couldn't bear to see destroyed.

"This was my last case," he declared.

"What?"

"The rough magic of detection I here abjure." He raised his walking stick to the level of his glaucous eyes, then brought it down hard on the floor. "I have failed as a detective, as a lover, and as a man."

"What about your writing?"

"I did my best writing thirty years ago. At this point it's an exercise in self-parody. I leave it to you to give the world an accurate account of this case. You must do so quickly, before Moreau can put a false narrative before the public. And you must write it so that I die in the end."

"So you die in the end?"

"As Don Quixote died. Otherwise Moreau will fill the bookstalls and libraries with spurious sequels, as Avellaneda did."

I had never seen Borges, or anyone else, in such a state of despair. I had to get him out of that house. "Wait here," I told him. "I'll go get our luggage so we can leave."

My last glance at him in that parlor seems a glimpse of frozen time, like one of those eternal moments before

Achilles's arrow reaches its target. He sat gripping his cane with both hands, his head bowed as if in final submission to his fate. That image will remain in my mind to the end of my days, no matter how much my memory fades.

9.

As Borges perceived, Maximilian Duke's demise owed little or nothing to the workings of fate. It came about through the exercise of free will: conscious actions of wicked, malevolent people, starting with the diabolical woman Borges claimed to love. How comforting it would have been to attribute her machinations to the irony of fate. But even Borges had to recognize that no such comfort could be his. He liked to say that he could see through the veil of appearances into the essence of things. But in this, his last case as a detective, his perception had been spectacularly wrong. His ideal woman's ugliness—invisible to his clouded eyes—was an accurate reflection of her depraved heart.

Alexandra Duke, as it turned out, was worse than he would ever know. Amid the hubbub following Moreau's arrest, she had been conspicuous by her absence. I put Borges in the car and went back to the house to look for her, trying to muster some appropriate words of farewell. What do you say to a hostess who has conspired with her lover to murder her husband and ducked out of sight as he was hauled off by the police?

It was Geneviève who met me at the door. As shocked and rattled as I'd been by the day's events, I found some glimmer of hope in her lovely blue eyes—something to warm the heart, if only in my next lifetime. "I want to thank you," I said, "for the role you played in solving the case. You're the one who told us about Jackson's attack on the man in Mexico."

"Yes," she nodded.

"And about what was going on between Max and Helen, and between Alexandra and Moreau. Without that information, Borges's investigation would have taken a much different course."

She was smirking, a little condescendingly, I thought, as if she couldn't believe how naive I was. "Glad to have done my part to make the weekend a success," she said.

That made me cringe. Was this a time for sarcasm? I tried to cut her some slack. After all, English wasn't her native language.

But she was laughing now. "Alexandra feels the same way."

"She does?" I could hardly believe what I was hearing. "Where is Alexandra, by the way?"

"Oh, she's right where she wanted to be as soon as Moreau was out of the way," Geneviève smiled. "Upstairs in bed with Trevor."

∞

Is this my memory speaking, or my imagination? Did all this really happen? Admittedly I added a few touches to the narrative, filled in a few gaps—how can you ever be sure that what you remember is the truth? Even where my recollections were clear and confident, I took some liberties for the sake of vividness and form. Maximilian Duke was even more obnoxious than I made him out to be, and his son a little less so. Professor Koenig was considerably less amusing than as I portrayed him, and Helen Rizzoli not quite as smart. I seem to recall a couple of other suspects who were dismissed early on; they were omitted in keeping with Borges's rule that a detective story can't involve more than six suspects. Poor Moreau did play the sap for Alexandra, I'm sure of that. The police questioned her and of course she denied any involvement in the murder; Moreau's claim that she promised to marry him was dismissed by the judge who sentenced him to life imprisonment in Walpole State Penitentiary. I recall that she married Trevor, the ex-pool boy, about a year later and that they moved to a villa in the south of France. Jackson was never heard from again.

I've put off writing this tale for over fifty years because I couldn't bring myself to let Borges die in the end. That would have violated one of his firmest rules for the detective story, which is essentially in the comic mode—the detective never dies. He did renounce detection, as he promised to do, returning to Argentina and the lovely Maria K., who soon became his wife. And with that he also gave up his Platonic pursuit of the ideal woman, having a real one at his side. He died peacefully at home in Geneva about ten years later, not in an insane asylum like Avellaneda's Don Quixote. In what must be counted as an ironic twist of fate (the last one in this tale), it was Moreau, not Borges, who ended his life in a madhouse. Apparently he was overheard expounding French literary theory in the prison cafeteria and was put in a strait jacket for his own protection. If he tried to write his own account of the Duke case it would have been dismissed as the ravings of a madman.

As I sit here I can practically feel my synapses locking down, millions at a time. I don't have many days left to be who I think I am. And then what? Is there any difference between Dante's oblivious souls in paradise and Nagarjuna's extinction of the self? We're all impostors, Borges said, pretending to be who we think we are. When enough synapses go, you give up pretending.

At that inevitable moment all my memories—and all my perceptions, my sensations, my desires, my happiness, my regrets—will have fled to the outer edge of the universe like the light from an extinguished star. Unbounded from this nutshell, I will count myself a king of infinite space. Borges lived on in my memory and now, dear reader, I hope to live on in yours, a Scheherazade kept alive through my stories. Just one word of advice: don't try to escape from the *mise en abîme*. You won't succeed. If this book is a dream, it's your dream as well as mine. Before you come to "The End"—it's just one page ahead—turn back to the beginning and read the whole thing through again. How do you know you won't vanish when the dream ends?

The End

Acknowledgements

The Philosophical Detective's Last Case is the third book in a trilogy, the two predecessors being *The Philosophical Detective* (first published in 2014) and *The Philosophical Detective Returns* (2020). I am indebted to the real Jorge Luis Borges (1899-1986), who was of course the original of the impostor featured in these books, and his marvelous works of fiction, non-fiction and poetry (many of which have been published in English translation by Penguin Books). As to the present book I would mention "Funes, the Memory," "The Immortals," "Shakespeare's Memory," "The Nothingness of Personality," "A New Refutation of Time," "Personality and the Buddha," "Partial Magic of the Quixote," and "When Fiction Lives in Fiction," which inspired parts of this book.

I would also like to acknowledge the many others whose writings on Borges, memory, physics, philosophy, and detective fiction have inspired or informed my writing, of which I can mention only a few: *Trent's Last Case,* by E.C. Bentley; *The Art of Memory,* by Frances A. Yates; *Helgoland,* by Carlo Rovelli; *Cosmological Koans,* by Anthony Aguirre; *The Message and the Book: Sacred Texts of the World's Religions,* by John Bowker; and a doctoral dissertation at the City University of New York, "The New Physics of Italo Calvino and Jorge Luis Borges" by Mark Thomas Rinaldi.

About the Author

Bruce Hartman is the author of ten previous novels, including *The Philosophical Detective* and *The Philosophical Detective Returns,* the first two books in the Philosophical Detective trilogy, which is now complete.

His first book, *Perfectly Healthy Man Drops Dead,* won the Salvo Press Mystery Novel Award and was published by Salvo Press in 2008. In 2018 it was republished in a slightly revised form by Swallow Tail Press. Bruce Hartman's books have ranged from mysteries (*The Rules of Dreaming, The Muse of Violence,* and the Philosophical Detective trilogy) to comedies (*A Butterfly in Philadelphia, Potlatch*), techno/political satire (*Big Data Is Watching You!*), a legal thriller (*The Devil's Chaplain*), and an action adventure (*Parole*). A graduate of Wesleyan University and Harvard Law School, he lives with his wife in Philadelphia.

Made in United States
Orlando, FL
23 May 2023

33411092R00131